Lunch Money Can't **SHOOT**

Lunch Money Can't SHOOT

MICHAEL LEVIN
New York Times Best Selling Author

& JACK PANNELL
Founder and organizer of the
Baltimore Collegiate School for Boys

NEW YORK

NASHVILLE • MELBOURNE • VANCOUVER

Lunch Money Can't **SHOOT**

This is a work of fiction. Names, characters, businesses, places, events, and incidents are either the products of the author's imagination or used in a fictitious manner. Any resemblance to actual persons, living or dead, or actual events is purely coincidental.

Published in New York, New York, by Morgan James Publishing. Morgan James is a trademark of Morgan James, LLC. www.MorganJamesPublishing.com

ISBN 978-1-68350-110-7 paperback
ISBN 978-1-68350-112-1 eBook
ISBN 978-1-68350-111-4 hardcover
Library of Congress Control Number: 2016908983

Cover Design by:
Rachel Lopez
www.r2cdesign.com

Interior Design by:
Bonnie Bushman
The Whole Caboodle Graphic Design

20% of all author income from the series will be donated to

Baltimore Collegiate School For Boys,
an African American charter school

Chapter 1

MEET LUNCH MONEY

"I'm hungry," William "Lunch Money" Barnes announced, as he stepped into the neat, attractive three-bedroom home he shared with his mother and his grandmother.

He tossed his backpack, as always, on the homework desk his mother had set up for him in the living room beneath the portrait of Rosa Parks. His grandmother gave him an amused smile as she carried a plate of chicken and rice to the dining room table.

"Mm, mm, mm," she clucked. "Don't they even feed you at that school of yours? You're the hungriest twelve-year-old I know!"

"I'm just a growing boy," William said happily, grinning and accepting a kiss from his grandmother.

"Did you lock the door?" she asked, as she always did.

"I locked the door," William said, as always delighted by the scent of his grandmother's awesome cooking. "Like always."

"As always," Beatrice corrected, gently rubbing his hair. "You need another haircut."

"First let me eat," he said, tearing into the food.

His Grandmama's chicken was better than any he'd ever tasted, so tender it fell right off the bone. To top it all off, she made rice with bits of bacon and collard greens. For Grandmama, cooking wasn't a hobby. It was an art.

His grandmother sat down beside him. With her right hand she swept the crumbs off the placemat, thinking for not the first time how every trail of breadcrumbs in that house led straight to the same source: her precious—if untidy—grandson.

At that moment, two of his friends leaned into the front window. "Lunch Money," one hollered, "come on out and play."

"I ain't playing 'til I finish eating," he shouted back.

"You keep saying *ain't* in my house," Beatrice cautioned, "and you *ain't* eating."

"All right then, Grandmama: *may* I go out and play *after I have finished* eating? Please and thank you?"

"What is it you're asking me? To go out and play in the pitch black when you should be safe inside, doing your homework?" She grunted a laugh. "Ask the pastor."

William rolled his eyes. That was her answer to practically any question he raised about what he could or could not do. "Ask the pastor" was Grandmama-speak for "No way, Jose."

"How come they call you that, anyway? 'Lunch Money'?" she asked, standing over him and watching him eat. Few things gave Beatrice more pleasure.

"Beats me," William said, trying to hide his embarrassment.

At that moment, his mother stepped out of the kitchen and into the dining room.

"Why *do* they call you that, son?" Adele Barnes asked.

"Mom!" William exclaimed, surprised. "How come you're home so early?"

"Parent-teacher thing tonight," she explained. "I'm bringing snacks. So why do they call you that?"

His Moms pulled out a chair and sat down opposite him. William could feel her eyes boring into him, searching out some kind of secret he did not want to reveal.

William's eyes darted around the downstairs rooms. He glanced at the iconic portraits of Civil Rights leaders and legends on the walls for help. Martin Luther King, Jr. Medgar Evers. Emmett Till. He knew them all. His grandmother had told him their stories every night when he was a little boy.

But none of them could help him now.

"It's just a name," William said, lowering his eyes and trying to concentrate on his food.

"I was born at night," Adele told him, and he knew exactly what she was going to say next. "But I wasn't born *last* night."

At moments like this, it was all William could do to keep himself from reciting the phrase along with her. But he knew that would not have done him any good.

"So why do they call you Lunch Money?" she repeated, eyes boring into her son.

"You'd do best to answer the question," Beatrice added, studying her grandson.

William gave her a pained look, as if to say, not you, too, Grandmama.

"If you must know," William said, and the usual smile on his face was suddenly nowhere to be seen.

"I must," Adele said, gently probing.

She could tell that something was upsetting William, because he stopped eating. After school, William *never* stopped eating until the plate was practically polished, it was so clean.

"There are these boys," he began, in a voice barely loud enough to be heard. He picked at his placemat as he spoke.

"By the projects," he continued, looking at his food as if he had no idea what food was for. His appetite was gone. He had to tell the whole truth.

"Every day, on my way to school, if I don't give them my Lunch Money, I get a beating."

Adele pursed her lips. She studied her son to determine whether he was telling the truth. William wasn't a very good liar so he didn't try lying often, at least not around his mother and Grandmama, who both seemed like human lie detectors. William looked directly into her eyes, as if to say, *you've got to believe me.*

Grandmama patted the pearls around her throat and cast her eyes heavenward. "Land sakes, child. So *that's* why you're always so hungry. Mm, mm, mm."

"The same three boys?" Adele asked, her piercing gaze leaving William nowhere to hide.

"Yes, ma'am," he said, lowering his eyes to his food.

"Every day?"

He nodded again. It was times like these when he really missed his father. Not that he had ever known his father. But if his father were around, he wouldn't be getting threatened by those boys every day and he wouldn't be getting cross-examined by his Moms.

"Do these boys go to school?" Adele asked.

"Not to my knowledge, ma'am," William said politely.

Adele thought for a moment. Her home was two blocks from a housing project that, as things went, wasn't the worst of its kind but wasn't the best, either. There were a lot of kids William's age who had already gotten into trouble, and in their neighborhood, trouble was never hard to find.

"Do you know what you're going to do?" Adele asked.

"Finish my chicken?" William asked hopefully.

"You'll finish your chicken when we get back," Adele said firmly. "Right now, we're going down to that project. And you're going to find me those three boys."

"What are you going to do?" William asked, and a smile crept over his face. "Beat them up?"

"Uh-uh," Adele said, shaking her head firmly. "*You* are."

Chapter 2

SOMETIMES YOU'D RATHER GET A BEATING

As Adele marched an unwilling William the two blocks from their home to the housing project, she realized that she had been dreading this moment ever since William was born. This was the moment when it became absolutely clear that the neighborhood was no longer safe enough for William to go to school.

Adele had grown up in the stately, Victorian home which had been part of a healthy, working class neighborhood for decades, until the drug man came to town. For decades, drugs had been the scourge of the neighborhood, tearing down the work ethic with its promise of easy money and good times. So many young men and women of the neighborhood had fallen prey to the world of drugs, either using them or worse, dealing them.

That group included William's father, who had gotten involved with drugs not long after William was born, had been arrested a few times for possession or dealing, and then fled for parts unknown.

He had never been heard from since.

The three of them lived in a home her maternal grandfather—Beatrice's father, a Pullman porter—had built with his own two hands. But the neighborhood had changed. Maybe it wasn't a safe enough place to raise William, especially without a father present. Boys were threatening her son every single day and taking his Lunch Money? To the point where he had actually gotten "Lunch Money" as a nickname? Not a good sign.

William wasn't exactly the happiest person in the world as his Moms took him down the two blocks to the projects. He was hoping against hope that the boys who bothered him would be somewhere else. If there was anything more embarrassing than a boy being walked down the street by his own mother, William had no idea what it might have been. And there they were, in the usual spot, on their park bench.

"Lunch Money!" called out the tallest with a happy grin as William and his mother approached. "We gonna double dip today? Your timing is perfect because I'm hungry all over again!"

William froze.

"Is that the boy?" Adele asked coolly.

William gave a small nod.

"Are those the other two?" she asked, pointing to his companions.

They all looked to be about fifteen or sixteen. They were all six feet tall. None of them looked as though they had seen the inside of a schoolroom for years. Their sneakers were gleaming, like the diamond studs in their ears.

"Which one do you want me to fight first?" William said quietly to his mother.

As if he had any serious idea of fighting any of them.

Adele considered her options. She could tell the young men off, which would humiliate William. Or she could...turn the other cheek.

No, not today.

Adele scowled at the three boys, whose mothers she knew from church. The boys lost some of their swagger when they realized Adele wasn't playing.

"Afternoon, Mrs. Barnes," one said meekly.

"Don't you hoodlums have any better place to be?" Adele snapped, and she faced the tallest boy. "Your name is Harold, right?"

"Yes, ma'am," he said, looking at the ground.

"And you're the Johnson twins, aren't you?" she said to the other two. "Does your mother know where you are right now?"

"Yes, ma'am," the second boy said, earning a sharp elbow in the ribs from his twin brother.

"We'll just be going along now," the second Johnson boy said.

"I know this is public property," Adele said, pointing to the bench they occupied, "but it's time for you to treat it like it's my living room. And you're not *invited*."

William slapped his forehead.

Adele glanced at him.

"I don't think these boys are going to bother you again," Adele told William.

"They're not going to bother me," William muttered. "They're going to *kill* me."

"I know your mamas from church," Adele told the three young men, not finished with them. "And none of you is too old to get a whuppin', from them or from me."

That was too much for William. He slapped his forehead again, turned, and started walking home.

"William," Adele called after him. "Don't you have anything you want to say to these hoodlums?"

"Um, have a nice day?" William asked.

This time, he ran for home, never looking back.

Chapter 3

OUTTA HERE!

By the time he got back to the house a few minutes later, William's appetite had grown as cold as the chicken and rice still sitting on the dining room table.

All he could think about was finding alternate ways to get to school. It was bad enough to get shaken down for your Lunch Money every day, to the point where people actually called you Lunch Money. It was another thing altogether for your Moms to have to go down and make a scene. *As if I couldn't stand up on my own two feet.*

Adele reached the house two minutes after William did. She nodded to Beatrice and the two women went into the kitchen without a word. William headed over to the homework table to start getting his math done. He could hear low, serious tones from the kitchen. That was never good. They only talked that way on the few occasions he had gotten himself into some sort of trouble.

He didn't get into much trouble—certainly nothing like the kind of trouble you could easily find in the neighborhood. But his Moms and his Grandmama had little tolerance for anything out of line. William had once heard a police officer at a school assembly talk about the "broken windows" school of policing. It meant that if you stopped people from doing little things—like breaking windows—then they wouldn't get around to doing big things like committing major crime.

William thought the concept sounded familiar.

It was how his Moms and Grandmama had raised him.

And besides, William was a good kid. He'd never broken a window in his life, at least not on purpose. Pop Warner football didn't count. He'd wanted to play Little League, but there was none in his area. His mother had long ago decided that if he was home studying, he couldn't be out in the streets getting into trouble. So he had to spend so much time studying that he never had enough time to play ball. As a result, the other kids his age were a million times better than he was at pretty much every sport.

Now he tried to focus on his math, without much luck. All he could think about was what his mother and grandmother were cooking up in the kitchen. And he knew it wasn't more chicken and rice.

A few minutes later, Adele emerged. She looked serious.

"What did I do?" William asked, staring at his mother. "I didn't do anything wrong!"

"No," Adele agreed, sadly shaking her head. "You didn't do anything wrong. *I* did. Trying to raise you here."

William cocked his head and studied her. "What's wrong with raising me here?" he asked, surprised. "This is our house!"

Adele shook her head and punched in a number on her cell phone.

"I'm calling your Uncle Ted," she said.

"Uncle Ted?" William asked, confused.

William had only met Uncle Ted a few times. He was the wealthiest member of the entire extended family. He made a lot of money in real estate, whatever that was. Something to do with collecting rent. William had heard Uncle Ted argue with his Moms at family gatherings that the neighborhood wasn't safe and that they needed to move out. His Moms had always disagreed, arguing back that she wasn't going to let "hoodlums" push her out of the house her grandfather built.

"Ted, it's Adele," she said. "Look, you were right and I was wrong. Do you still have that house?"

"What house?" William asked cautiously.

Adele gave him a look like, don't even talk to me right now.

"No? Well, where's the other one?" Adele asked.

She listened.

William waited.

"Fifty *miles?* I can't drive that far to work...I guess the boy could live with his grandmother during the week and I could join them on weekdays, at least until I get transferred. Yes. We'll take it."

She hung up and turned to William.

"Pack your bags," she said, and it sounded to William as though she was trying to keep the emotion out of her voice. "I can't raise you among the hoodlums here."

"Moving?" he asked, staring at her. "Is that really… *necessary*?"

"It's not just necessary," his mother told him, shaking her head. "It's long overdue."

"When are we going to move?" William asked.

His mother shrugged.

"Right now," she said. "Unless you're planning on getting shaken down for your Lunch Money again tomorrow."

William thought about it.

"Well, when you put it that way," he said with a shrug.

Two hours later, the car was packed with William's clothing and schoolbooks and Beatrice's frying pan and other vital kitchen items, and they were on their way.

Chapter 4

THE NEW NEIGHBORHOOD

An hour later, Adele was driving through an unfamiliar neighborhood fifty miles south of the city that William, in the backseat, and Beatrice, in the passenger seat, would now call home. William's eyes were glued out the window.

"This place is *nice*," he said, looking at the attractive houses, the manicured lawns, and the cars parked in driveways.

"Mm-hmm," Adele said absentmindedly, trying to find street numbers on the houses.

"There's not a single car up on blocks," William marveled. "These people must be rich!"

"Hush your mouth," said Grandmama. "Don't talk like you've been raised in some kind of ghetto! We never had *our* car up on blocks."

"Yeah but remember when I was little how I thought the blocks were just an extension of a car's wheels?"

Silence. William looked in the rearview mirror and saw his mother set her jaw. In the passenger seat, Grandmama fingered her pearls like she always did when she was mad or anxious. Had he said something wrong? William thought it was a funny memory, but it didn't seem so funny now.

"There it is," Adele said suddenly, and she turned quickly into the driveway of a moderately sized, beautiful two-story house. Could've used a little fresh paint, but aside from that, William thought, it was fantastic. Much bigger than the house he had known in the city. On top of that, there were similar houses stretched out in every direction.

Not a housing project in sight.

"Guess I'll get to keep my Lunch Money around here," he said.

"Don't worry about that," Adele said, turning off the engine. "Please bring in the suitcases."

"Yes, ma'am," William said.

He grappled with the bags while his Moms and Grandmama walked into the house and gave it an inspection. Uncle Ted said he hadn't had time to get it cleaned, but it didn't look that bad. The previous tenants, whoever they were, had left the place in decent shape. Even Grandmama had nothing to complain about. The first thing she did, after William had brought in all the belongings, was to find a hammer and nails in the garage.

She promptly put up the portraits of Dr. Martin Luther King, Jr., Rosa Parks, Medgar Evers, and Emmett Till.

"*Now* this place looks like a home," she said approvingly. William couldn't help but admire how adept his grandmother was with a hammer. She possessed the same grace hammering those nails into the wall as when she fluttered over the stove at dinner, stirring each pot with a different spatula.

William took his own suitcase, brought it upstairs, and found himself in a bedroom twice as big as any he had ever seen. He unpacked his clothing into the furniture, which looked reasonably new, and thought this might work out. When he came downstairs, his mother and grandmother were waiting for him at the dining room table.

"What did I do this time?" he asked, seeing the stern looks on their faces.

"You haven't done anything," his mother said. "It's just that...well...your grandmother and I have to tell you a little bit about the facts of life."

William nearly choked on his mouthful of food.

"The facts of *life*?" he repeated, squirming in his seat. "Can't Uncle Ted tell me about that? I'd rather hear that from a guy."

His mother laughed. "Not those facts of life, dear," she said, reaching out and squeezing his hand. "And you're right, Uncle Ted would be much better for that conversation. I just wanted to talk to you about life here in Turnberry."

"What's there to know?" William asked happily. "It's beautiful! Our house is twice as nice. The neighborhood's twice as nice. I'm sure *everything's* going to be twice as nice."

William watched his mother and grandmother exchange concerned glances.

"There's one thing that's different here, William," his grandmother said.

"Like what?" William asked.

"Uncle Ted told me," Adele began, choosing her words carefully, "that there aren't any...people like us here."

William pondered the words.

"You mean everybody's married and stuff?" he asked.

Adele gave a small sigh.

"I'm sure many of the people are," she said. "But that's not what I'm getting at."

"Lord in heaven," Beatrice said, shaking her head. "Just come right out and say it, honey. The truth never hurt a flea." She turned and looked squarely at William. "Your mother's trying to tell you that everybody here is white."

William blinked.

"Is that true?" he asked, processing the surprising fact. "We're the only black family in town?"

"That's what Uncle Ted said," Adele said. "I just hope we're not going from the frying pan into the fire. Those hoodlums shaking you down for your Lunch Money weren't exactly my cup of tea. But at least they're our people."

"Hoodlums aren't *my* people," William countered, "no matter what color they are. A hoodlum is a hoodlum."

"Well," Adele said cautiously, "white people are...different. And they may never have met African Americans before."

"Really?" William said. "You've got to be kidding me."

"We have no way of knowing, son. So I just want you to be prepared."

"Just 'cause they white, don't mean they right," Beatrice said quietly.

Adele glared at her. "That's not the message we're trying to give William right now," she said, being careful about how she rebuked her mother in front of her son. "And anyway, when did the Queen of Good Grammar relinquish her crown?"

Beatrice flushed a little, then reached for her pearls and stroked them thoughtfully. "You're right. About the grammar, anyway."

Adele turned back to her son. "William, all I'm trying to say is that, well, you just want to be careful."

"Careful how?" William asked thoughtfully. "I've met white people before. They're just...people. Aren't they?"

Adele took her son's hand.

"Of course they're just people," she said. "But not all of them *like* us. They may not take kindly to us just moving into their community. You just have to be on your guard. That's all I'm saying."

"On my guard for what?" William asked, increasingly confused. "They're gonna let me eat lunch, won't they? I think I have less to look out for here than I did back in the city."

"It may be more subtle here," Adele said, and it looked as if her heart were breaking. "I just hope we're doing the right thing. I've had my doubts for a long time about the way our neighborhood was going. I just didn't want to take a chance on anything bad happening to you. You're my only son."

"And you're my only Moms," William said, giving Adele a big smile and squeezing her hand. "I'm not afraid of white people. I'm not afraid of anybody! Except maybe Grandmama when she starts chasing me around the house with that big 'ol frying pan of hers."

"I've never done any such thing!" Beatrice said indignantly. "If I ever run after you, it's only to sweep up that ever-lovin' trail of crumbs you leave behind!"

"I was just kidding, Grandmama," William said. "So what do I have to know about white people if I'm going to fit in over here?"

"Typically, black people have to work twice as hard just to get the same rewards and results that white people get," Adele said.

"Mm, mm. They might smile at you," Beatrice added, "but that doesn't mean they really want to be your friend."

"In a place like this," Adele said, "where they've maybe never seen black folk before, I don't know what they're going to think of us."

"One day, black won't have to get back," Grandmama said. "Yellow will be mellow. White will be all right. But until then..."

"You make white people sound scarier than hoodlums," William said.

They all laughed.

Suddenly the doorbell rang, and everybody stared at each other.

"Look through the peephole," Adele cautioned William, who got up to answer the door.

William looked out the window before he got to the door. He turned back to his mother and grandmother.

"It's just some kids," he said.

"White kids, I reckon," Beatrice said. "Mm, mm, mm. Here's where the rubber meets the road."

William opened the door.

Two white kids William's age, one with the reddest hair William had ever seen, and the other with brown hair and blue eyes, stood at the doorway. The one with red hair was tall and skinny and holding a basketball.

"We saw you just moved in," the one with red hair said. "We just wanted to know if you wanted to come shoot some hoops with us."

William's eyes widened.

He looked back at his mother and grandmother for guidance and permission.

Neither of them knew what to say.

"We're just going to the schoolyard down the block," the one with brown hair and blue eyes said. He was much shorter than his friend, with big round freckles across his nose and cheeks. He seemed to be the one in charge, or at very least the one assessing the situation. He sensed Adele's hesitation and waved a friendly hello.

"No need to worry, Mrs. . . ."

"Barnes," Adele said, filling in the blank.

"Mrs. Barnes. No need to worry about your son. We've lived here forever. It's a super safe neighborhood." He turned back to William. "Come hang out with us."

Adele seemed satisfied. "Fine with me, as long as you're home before it gets dark."

Red peered into the living room where he saw the portraits of the Civil Rights leaders.

"Are those relatives?" he asked innocently.

William studied the red-haired one, trying to see if he was making fun of him. He then glanced at his mother and grandmother. They were both mystified.

"They're kind of relatives," he allowed.

"Cool. You like Madden?" the red-haired boy asked William.

"You like Xbox?" asked the boy with brown hair and blue eyes.

"I like both," said William.

"I'm Tommy," said the boy with brown hair and blue eyes. "Tommy O'Connell."

"I'm Fred, but everybody calls me Red," said the kid with red hair. He pointed to his head. "You can probably see why."

"My name's William," William said, "but all my friends call me Lunch Money."

The boys smiled. "Lunch Money? That's a funny name!"

"There's a story behind it," William told them as he headed out the door to shoot hoops.

"Your name is William!" Adele shouted after him. "And be home by—"

William didn't hear what time he was supposed to be home by, because he was already out the door with his new friends.

If these are white people, William thought, as he headed to the schoolyard with them, *I think things might just be all right.*

Chapter 5

H-O-R-S-E

Red bounced the ball as he, Tommy, and William headed down the sidewalk to the schoolyard. It was early evening, the streets were empty of cars and other people, and William was struck by just how *quiet* everything was.

"So where are you from?" Red asked.

"The city," William said, not sure just how specific he should be. There were some nice parts of the city and some not-so-nice parts. He came from one of the not-so-nice parts. How much was he supposed to tell them?

It's just an innocent question, he thought, *but still.*

"Uh-huh," Red said.

Apparently that was all the information they needed.

Interesting, William thought.

"How come you moved?" Tommy asked.

William thought before he spoke. He didn't want to tell the boys about how he had been shaken down for his Lunch Money. It was too embarrassing. Besides, he didn't want to give them the same idea.

"My Moms wanted to," William said.

"Your *moms*?" Red asked, glancing at William with surprise. "You have two moms? Were those the two people in your house?"

William, confused, shook his head.

"I only have one Moms," he said. "The other person is my Grandmama."

Red gave a nod of understanding, even though he didn't entirely understand. Tommy gave Red a look as if to say, Come on, get with the program—don't you watch TV?

"So the three of you live together," Tommy said. "Your mother, your grandmother, and you."

"Yup," William said, as they reached the schoolyard. "My Moms—my *mother*—still has a job up in the city. Until she can transfer and work down here, it'll be my Grandmama—I mean my *grandmother*—and me here and my...*mother* will come down for the weekends."

William wasn't quite sure how the other boys would react to the idea of living with a grandmother, but to his surprise, they liked it.

"You're so lucky," Red said, as they stepped onto the school grounds. "Grandmothers are cool. They don't make you do anything. They just feed you snacks while you sit around gaming."

"Not *my* grandmother," William said, taking in the school and schoolyard with an admiring gaze. "She makes me do *everything.*"

"This is our school," Tommy said. "I guess you'll be going here, too."

"I suppose," William said, looking around, surprised. "Hey, there's no fence!"

Tommy and Red looked at each other. "Fence for what?" Tommy asked, as the boys walked toward the basketball court. Red dribbled all the while.

"To keep the hoodlums out," William said, and Tommy and Red laughed, which only confused William further. He glanced quickly at each of them.

"We don't really have hoodlums around here," Tommy said, smiling. "Except maybe Red. A lot of people say he's a hoodlum."

"They do not!" Red replied indignantly. "*You're* a hoodlum!"

"We have some mean kids," Tommy said, frowning and passing William the ball. "There's this guy Martin on the basketball team. But nobody who's really, like, a *bad* kid. If you know what I mean."

William nodded, as if he knew exactly what Tommy meant. He searched his memory to see if he had ever seen a school that didn't have fencing for the precise purpose of keeping hoodlums, drug dealers, and other undesirables away from the school kids. But this school had no fence whatsoever. *Maybe they couldn't afford a fence*, he thought.

And yet, the school looked pretty new, compared with his school back in the neighborhood. In fact, it looked so new that William wondered if it had just opened this year.

"Everybody hates this place," Tommy said, noticing that William was staring at the school. "Everybody says it's like jail. But me? I look at it as a playground of opportunity. It's just a training ground for the next big thing."

He cocked his head to the side, sizing up his new short friend who seemed to be a budding philosopher with freckles.

"Heads up!" Red passed William the basketball and he dribbled it a couple of times. He couldn't believe how well it bounced. It was the newest basketball he had ever held.

"Doesn't look like any jail *I've* ever heard of," William murmured. "What are all these empty fields for?"

Tommy and Red looked surprised.

"It's where we play during recess," Tommy said. "Soccer. Flag football. Softball. Whatever season it is, that's what game we play."

"What's flag football?" William asked.

The boys glanced at him again, as if he had come not from another planet. "You know, dude," Red said. "Where you've got flags on a belt and the guy has to grab your flag."

William shook his head. The only football he knew was tackle. People actually carried around flags while they were playing football? How could they catch passes? He didn't want to look stupid, so he didn't ask any more questions about flag football.

"Put it up, Lunch Money," Red said in a teasing yet friendly voice. "Let's see what you've got."

"Huh?" William asked, his thoughts disrupted by the idea of actually playing basketball. At least it took his mind off flag football, whatever *that* was. "Okay."

William dribbled a few more times, paused, and made ready to shoot.

That's when he noticed the basketball hoops had something he had never seen on a playground in his community.

They had nets.

"Nets," he blurted out.

Once again, Tommy and Red glanced at him with puzzled expressions on their faces.

"Is that a game?" Red asked. "Nets? How do you play Nets?"

"We play Horse," Tommy said.

William shook his head.

"There are nets," he said, nodding at the hoops. "On the rims. What are they, like, nylon?"

Both boys shrugged. They had no idea what the nets were made of. Of course there were nets on basketball hoops.

"Looks like the NBA," William marveled.

"Whatever," Red said impatiently. "Come on, Lunch Money, shoot."

William looked at the net, bounced the ball a couple more times, measured his shot, and clanged it off the rim.

"Shoot again," Tommy said kindly. He caught the ball on a rebound and passed it back to William.

"Okay," William said. He measured, fired...and missed again. This time he hit the backboard but not the rim.

"One more," Tommy said, and bounced back toward William.

William, flushed, took the ball, dribbled it a couple of times, and chucked it up toward the basket. He didn't even dare look to see if it went in. But then he looked.

It did.

"Nothing but net," Red said, in a friendly way, as if he were announcing the shot on TV.

"Nothing to it," William said, but inwardly he was deeply relieved. He thought he was never going to make a shot.

"Let's play Horse," Tommy said.

"Okay," William said.

"I'll go first."

Tommy took the basketball and stood at the edge of the circle past the line for shooting foul shots. He fired...and scored.

"Nice shot," William said, rebounding the ball and pushing it out toward Red.

Red took it, went to the same spot at the top of the key, dribbled, dribbled again, and fired. He made the shot.

"Good one," William said.

Tommy bounce passed him the ball. William went to the same spot, fired, and missed everything. Air ball.

"You've got H," Tommy said.

Tommy took the ball and went to a spot about eighteen feet from the basket on the left-hand side. "That's his shot," Red told William. "Never let him get open over there."

William nodded seriously, as if he was filing away that information for the future.

Tommy dribbled once, measured the arc of his shot with his eyes, fired, and nailed it. *Wow*, William thought. *He may be short, but he's got game.*

Though William had only known him for half an hour, he got the impression Tommy thought about the arc and angle of every shot before he made it. He seemed like one of those people whose mind was always spinning along at 100mph.

Tommy got his own rebound and kicked it out to Red, who dribbled the ball to the same spot, fired, and sunk his shot.

Red tossed the rebound to William.

William missed. Not by much—this time he hit the backboard and the rim, at least—but it didn't come all that close to going in.

"You've got O," Red said. And so it went. Tommy won, with Red one shot behind him. William only made one shot the whole game.

It was starting to get dark.

"I should be getting home soon," William said, embarrassed by his poor performance.

"You're just rusty," Red said, bounce-passing him the ball as they headed off school grounds and back toward their street.

"Maybe the hoops are a different height from what you were used to," Tommy said in a friendly voice. "They're higher, or lower, or something."

William, sensitive to being teased, studied each boy in turn, but he realized they were being sincere.

He was a new kid in town, and they were just trying to make him feel comfortable.

That's not what Moms and Grandmama said about white people, he realized. Or maybe there's something deeper going on.

But somehow he knew there wasn't.

He knew they were just kids.

"You said you guys grew up here?" William asked.

Both boys nodded. "We've both been going to that same school since kindergarten," Tommy said.

"Have either of you...ever been to the city?"

The boys thought for a moment.

"On a field trip," Red said.

"To the planetarium," Tommy said. "Last year. That's the day I decided I wanted to become an astronaut."

William smiled. Here was a point of common ground among them.

"I've been to the planetarium!" William said. "It's cool."

Both boys nodded. William wondered what they would think if they ever saw his neighborhood. It would probably blow their minds.

The boys reached William's house.

"You starting school tomorrow?" Tommy asked William.

William shrugged. "I suppose," he said. "I guess I have to enroll and all that kind of thing."

"Tell them you want to be in 6W," Tommy said. "That's our homeroom. That way you'll at least know some people."

"Yeah, hoodlums like us," Red said, flashing a grin. He spun the basketball on one of his long bony fingers. "Hoodlums holla!"

"You ain't hoodlums," William assured them. "Not even baby gangsters. Trust me."

"Be cool, Lunch Money," Tommy said, as William headed up the flagstones to his new front door. "Check you in the morning."

William nodded. "Thanks for the game," he said. "I'll do better next time."

"No doubt," Tommy said.

The boys gave William a little nod and continued down the path toward their own homes.

William stood on his new front porch, replaying the whole experience in his mind.

They seemed okay.

He watched them go.

Chapter 6

SHINY AND NEW

As soon as William rang the doorbell—his grandmother had locked the door the moment he had left, as a precaution—he could hear his mother stepping quickly to the door to unlock it and let him in.

She looked worried.

"How was it?" she asked, and she studied William from his hair to his gym shoes.

"I only went to play basketball," William reminded her, surprised by his mother's concern. "It's not like I went to Iraq or something."

His mother sighed. "You're right," she said. She put her arm around William and ushering him into the house. "A mother worries, that's all."

William looked around the house, trying to remember where the kitchen was.

"I'm hungry," he said. "And no, they didn't take my Lunch Money."

"I haven't had time to do any grocery shopping," Adele said apologetically as she followed him into the kitchen. "I don't even know where the stores are."

"Where's Grandmama?" William asked, opening the refrigerator and peering inside. It was practically empty. Some baking soda, whatever that was, and two cans of soda.

"Upstairs cleaning," Adele said. "Should we go to the supermarket?"

"Do you think they serve black people?" William asked sarcastically.

Adele closed her eyes and shook her head. "You're right," she said. "Maybe I'm being a little overprotective."

"They're just kids," William said, looking his mother in the eye. "They only wanted to play ball. It wasn't a Klan rally."

"Don't get fresh with me," Adele said, and then she relented and rubbed his hair. "I'll get my purse. We need food."

William grinned, the tension broken.

"Sounds good to me!" he exclaimed.

Five minutes later, Adele and William were in her car, headed to the market. Neither had any idea where it was, so William found directions to a supermarket on his mother's phone.

"I think you were more worried about me here with those two white kids than you ever were in our neighborhood," William said, watching the houses go by.

The houses were nice but not flashy. The cars were fairly new, mostly Japanese, mostly SUVs. The streets were almost empty. Nobody was walking around.

"Where is everybody?" William said. "Everybody here's going to bed. In our neighborhood, things would be just heating up."

Adele shrugged as she followed the directions of the GPS. "It's the suburbs," she explained. "People go home and stay home."

"Sounds boring," William said.

Adele nodded. "A little boring is just what we need," she said.

"Wow! Look at that!" William suddenly exclaimed.

They turned the last corner and came upon a supermarket the size of a football stadium.

"It's almost as big as a Wal-Mart," William marveled. "I guess white people eat a lot."

"You can make those jokes with me," Adele cautioned, "but you'd best be polite when you're out of my sight."

William had heard that line before. Too many times to count.

"I am," he said. "Look at this parking lot! It's so smooth! Looks like nobody's ever parked here! When did they build this town, last week?"

"It all does look new," Adele said. "New is nice. But I prefer lived-in."

William nodded. "I know what you mean," he said, as Adele steered the car into one of what seemed like hundreds of parking spaces. They headed toward the store.

"How long are we going to stay here?" William asked. "And don't tell me forever."

"Nothing's forever," Adele said as they entered the store and looked around. It was vast.

"Looks like you need to leave breadcrumbs to find your way back to the front," William said. "Seriously, Moms, how long are we going to stay here?"

"I have no idea," Adele said. "We'll just take it a day at a time. Get me a cart, will you?" William nodded and took a cart from the rack. He marveled at it.

"This thing has wheels like NASCAR," he exclaimed. "This shopping cart's probably faster than half the cars in our neighborhood."

He looked at all the other carts. "Shiny and new," he said, shaking his head in amazement. "Not a single one looks dented. How come white people get all the nice shopping carts and we get all the beat-up ones?"

"I love *our* neighborhood," Adele said, looking around and trying to get her bearings in the enormous store. "But people don't always take care of things the right way where we live."

William nodded. "It just seems like such a big store and there's almost nobody in it," he said, looking around. "Just like the streets. Maybe nobody's moved here yet. Maybe Tommy, Red, and I are gonna be the only three kids in the school."

Adele shook her head.

"When you get out of the city," she explained, "you've got more choices. More stores. More everything. So people can shop where they want to, not where they want to. My goodness! Look at these prices!"

William gave his mother a knowing look. "Way higher, right?" he asked. "I bet they jack everything up here to pay for all those shopping carts and parking spaces."

Adele shook her head. "This makes me so mad," she said quietly. "Everything here is so much cheaper than where we live."

William shot her a puzzled look. "How come? That's not right."

"It's not right," Adele said. "But it's reality. When you've got people who can only walk to the nearest market, you can charge them whatever you want. Where people have choices, and they can drive to places, you have to compete. These prices might be a third less than what we pay. Makes me so mad."

"You ought to be smiling, Mama," William said, putting his arm around his mother. "Look how much money we're going to save living here!"

"That's my boy," Adele said. "Always looking on the bright side."

"That's my Moms," William said, giving her a kiss on the cheek. "Always open to hearing my perspective. By the way, Mom, don't you have to get back to the city? You've got to get to work in the morning."

Adele shook her head. "I've got to register you for school in the morning," she said. "I already called in and told them I'd be late."

"I guess now that we're shopping white people prices," William said, a mischievous grin crawling across his face, "we can double up on these chocolate chip cookies. Look at that! So inexpensive! I think I'll take three bags!"

Adele shook her head and laughed. "Okay, young man," she said. "Now that I know that you'll get to eat them and not those hoodlums on that park bench!"

"Moms, they only took my money," William assured her. "Not my food."

Adele rolled her eyes. "Well, that's a relief," she said sarcastically.

"So I guess I'll take one more bag!" William said, and he tossed another bag of chocolate chip cookies into the cart. "Man, suburban living!" he exclaimed. "I think I could get used to this!"

They paid for their groceries and then headed home, if you can call a house you've lived in for less than two hours "home." William went to bed, but it took him a long time to fall asleep. He just couldn't imagine how a school could have nets on its baskets and no nets around the playground. What *was* this place, anyway?

Chapter 7

ON THE TEAM

The next morning, Adele and William headed out of the house and walked the two short blocks to school in order to get William registered.

William stared at his mother. "Moms, you look like you're dressed for church!" he exclaimed.

Adele self-consciously glanced at her outfit. She was indeed wearing one of her nicest dresses.

"Do you think I overdid it?" she asked. William was unfamiliar with the touch of self-doubt in her voice. His mother was typically the most confident, straight-ahead woman he had ever known.

"You look perfect," he reassured her. "You just look like you're nervous as a snitch at a gangster party."

Adele swallowed hard.

"You're right," she said. "And I don't know why I am. I'm sure the people are going to be lovely."

"Grandmama makes it sound like they're gonna eat me alive," William said cheerfully. "I think she's exaggerating again."

"She just wants you to be safe," Adele said, as they turned the corner and reached the school grounds.

Suddenly the streets that had been so empty the night before were teeming with life. Cars were dropping off kids, kids were walking to school by themselves, bicycling, skateboarding—it was as if the whole town had finally come to life.

"I feel a lot safer here than I did in the neighborhood," William said. "This looks like a place where it's against the law to break the law."

Adele nodded. She felt self-conscious. They were the only people of color in the entire stream of children and adults heading toward the school.

"Do you think we did the right thing?" she whispered to William. "Moving here?"

He grinned and patted her hand.

"We?" he asked in a teasing voice. "I think this decision was made entirely by you."

"Oh, William," Adele sighed.

"But unless I'm totally misreading the situation," he said happily, "it looks like I'm gonna get to eat my lunch today in peace!"

Adele flashed back on the hoodlums at the park bench in front of the housing project.

"I hope so," she said, still sounding uncertain.

They entered the building and got a welcoming smile from a friendly looking white man wearing a shirt and tie.

"Morning," Adele said politely to him.

He kept smiling, which seemed odd to both Adele and William. His expression suggested that he looked a little confused to see them.

"We're here to fix the air conditioning," William assured him.

"William!" his mother said indignantly, smiling all the while at the friendly man in the shirt and tie. "Don't say those things!"

"He looked like he was wondering why we're here," William said.

They took a few steps inside the school, which was unlike any school William had ever seen. It was so new looking, it looked like it had been built an hour ago. Paint was fresh. There was no litter. Everyone was proceeding at a fast pace in an orderly way to...well...somewhere. Wherever William looked, he saw signs announcing extracurricular activities—school plays, music groups, sports activities, PTA notices.

"Man, this place is *busy*," he marveled. "We don't have half that stuff at my school. We don't have *any* of it."

He realized something was missing.

"Where's the metal detector?" he asked, looking around. "Never heard of a school without a metal detector. Kids might be *carrying*. How you gonna know without a metal detector?"

At that moment, an older woman in a print dress approached Adele and William, who clearly looked as though they had no idea where they were going.

"May I help you?" she asked sweetly.

Too sweetly, Adele thought. Something inside her clenched.

"We're here to register my son for school," she said, politely but resolutely.

"Oh!" the woman exclaimed, and it seemed to both William and Adele that she was trying to cover her confusion with false enthusiasm. "Wonderful! Right this way!"

The woman led them through the throngs of students toward the school office.

"They'll help you," she said, leaving Adele and William standing at the barrier. On the other side were two women typing away, just as you would find in any school office anywhere.

Adele waited for one of them to look up. After a few minutes during which time neither looked up, Adele cleared her throat.

The women looked up.

"I'm here to register my son for school," Adele said politely.

The women gave Adele and William a puzzled look. One stood up.

"Right this way," she said, studying them with a surprised look on her face. "Principal Schmidt is still greeting the students. You can wait in his office."

She ushered them into the principal's office, which was pretty much like principals' offices everywhere—a globe, a map of the world, a desk with a lot of files on it, and photos of famous Americans on the wall.

Almost all of them were white.

Adele and William sat quietly opposite the principal's desk.

"Mm, mm, mm," William said. "Haven't been in school five minutes and already in the principal's office. Not a good start."

Adele rolled her eyes.

A few moments later, Principal Schmidt bustled in. It was the same guy who had been standing out front, greeting the students.

Adele rose to her feet. William followed suit.

"Well, if it isn't the young man here to fix the air conditioning," Principal Schmidt said. "How may I help you? Please have a seat."

"Don't mind my son," Adele said, smoothing her skirt out of nervousness. "He doesn't mean any harm."

"I can see he's a fine young man," the principal said. "How may I help you?"

"We're here to register," Adele said. "We just moved into the neighborhood."

The principal, who looked to William more like a guy you'd see on a cable TV show about camping, because of his slightly longish blond hair and outdoorsy look, gave a nod.

"Wonderful," he said seriously. "You're most welcome here. And your name is?"

"Lunch Money," William said.

Adele scowled. "His name is William Barnes," she informed the principal.

"But most people call me Lunch Money," William said affably.

"Sounds like I ought to call you William when your mother's here," the principal said, smiling. "And Lunch Money when she isn't. Is that correct?"

"You're the principal," William said, smiling back. "I guess that means you can call me whatever you want."

Inwardly, Adele was seething, but she did her best to keep a smile planted on her face.

"How soon can my son start school?" Adele asked. "I'm sure there's paperwork."

"There are some forms," the principal said. "By the way, my name is Dave Schmidt. But you can call me Principal Schmidt."

William liked the man's easy familiarity. Principal Schmidt wasn't nearly as stern as any of the principals he had known in his schools. They were serious men. They had to be. *I guess things are different here in the suburbs.*

"What kind of forms do we need?"

"Nothing major," Principal Schmidt said. "Transcripts for the last two years, immunization, proof of residency. We have really great schools in our town, and a lot of people claim to live here just so they can get their kids in."

Adele looked up quickly at him.

"Not that I would ever think you did that," he assured her.

Adele studied him. He seemed sincere. She let it go.

"I'm afraid we don't have any of those things with us," she admitted. "We just moved in last night."

"That's too bad," Principal Schmidt said, making his fingers into a little temple. "How long do you think it'll take to get all those things in order?"

Adele shook her head nervously.

"I have no idea," she admitted. "I don't know how long it's going to take William's last school to get transcripts to you. As for proof of residency, as I said, we just moved in last night. My brother owns the house. It'll probably take a few weeks to get the electricity put in our name."

"Well," Principal Schmidt said, "we don't want William missing any more school than he has to. But the nurse won't let him in without his immunization record."

"You mean shots?" William asked, suddenly nervous. "I gotta get shots to get in this school? Let's go home! All of a sudden those hoodlums on the park bench are looking really good to me!"

Adele gave her son a baleful look.

"You've already had your immunizations, son," she said. "I just have to call the doctor's office and get them to fax over the records. We could probably have that today."

"I think you're both going to like our school very much," Principal Schmidt said. "We have great teachers, fairly small classes for a public school, and terrific extracurricular activities. Do you like sports, William?"

"I like Madden," William said.

Principal Schmidt grinned. "I like Madden, too," he said. "I'm pretty good. Maybe I'll challenge you to a game at some point."

William raised his eyebrows. He had never heard of a principal playing Madden. To his knowledge, principals never played *anything*.

"I meant, do you like to *play* sports?" Principal Schmidt said. "You like basketball?"

"Are you asking me because I'm black?" William asked.

The principal blushed.

Adele gasped.

William just grinned.

"Just messing with you," William said. "Of course I like basketball. I'm not very good, though. Last night two boys from your school had no problem beating me playing Horse."

"You already met some kids?" Principal Schmidt asked. "That's wonderful. Who are they?"

"One kid who calls himself Red," William said, remembering, "and the other kid is Tommy. O'Connell, I think. I liked them. They were nice. But when it came to basketball, they beat me like a drum. I like to play, but I'm really not that good."

Principal Schmidt turned approvingly toward Adele. "This young man is very well-raised," he said. "I admire his humility. I'm sure he's quite good."

Because he's black, Adele thought, but she said nothing. Instead, she just nodded thanks for the compliment.

Principal Schmidt rubbed his chin and thought for a moment. "Your timing is just a little bit off," he said. "Basketball tryouts ended last night."

He studied William for a few moments and then his eyes lit up. He picked up the phone, pushed a button, and said, "Get Coach Clark in here right now," he said, with an authoritativeness that surprised both Adele and William. "I think I just found his new point guard."

"My son is here to learn, not to play ball—" Adele began, but the principal wasn't listening.

"Just a minute," the principal said. "I want you to meet Coach Clark. He coaches pretty much all our sports—basketball, football, baseball, track. We have decent teams, but we've never won a championship. I think the coach would be very excited to meet you."

William looked puzzled. "But I just told you," he said, confused. "I'm really not that good. I'm not being modest. When we choose up sides in my neighborhood, I get picked last. If at all."

The principal nodded approvingly at Adele. "Humility," he said firmly. "An excellent trait in a young man."

Adele didn't know what to say, but suddenly the doorway was filled with a very large man in sweatpants with a whistle around his neck.

Adele and William rose.

"This is Coach Clark," the principal said. "Coach, I think I found your new point guard."

Coach Clark, a sandy-haired, slightly overweight man who looked to be in his fifties, studied Adele for a moment and then William for a much longer period of time.

"Are you new?" he asked.

"We are," Adele said. "We're here to register my son."

"Forgive my manners," the principal said. "This is Mrs. Barnes."

Adele nodded, and she shook the coach's extended hand.

"And this is her son William, but you can call him Lunch Money."

The coach grinned.

"But only when my Mama's not around," William said. "Those times, you have to call me William."

The coach and William shook hands.

"Please have a seat," the coach said. "So you like to play point guard?" he asked, studying William's build.

"I like to play basketball," he said. "But like I keep telling the principal here, I'm really not that good."

"We have our first practice after school today," Coach Clark said. "Can you be there?"

"We don't have our paperwork," Adele said. "It's going to take me a few days—"

"I think we can finesse the paperwork for now," Principal Schmidt said.

"What does 'finesse' mean?" William asked.

"It means that we can kind of let that go," the principal said.

"Because I'm black?" William asked quietly.

Principal Schmidt and Coach Clark looked horrified.

Adele looked embarrassed.

"No, it's because you're a point guard," Coach Clark explained, recovering quickly. "Athletes always get special treatment."

"I'm not an athlete," William insisted, surprised that the men did not believe him.

"'Course you are," the coach said, smiling. And then, to Adele: "He's not boastful at all. Very well raised."

"Thank you," Adele said, and she didn't know whether to be pleased by the compliment or insulted by the implication that because William was African-American, he might not have been well-raised.

Adele was simply too overwhelmed to draw conclusions about what the principal was saying. "You mean William can start school today?" she asked.

Principal Schmidt shrugged.

"As long as he can make the practice after school," he said, "and I'm sure you can just get the paperwork filed quickly. I'll talk to the nurse and his guidance counselor."

Adele was speechless.

William grinned.

"Where's my easy button when I need it?" he asked Principal Schmidt. "I'm very excited to matriculate at your school. It looks like an excellent educational environment."

Principal Schmidt nodded approvingly.

"Your son is very well-spoken, too," he said happily. "I'm sure you'll do great here, William."

"Practice starts at three-thirty, but get there half an hour early, so you can be issued a uniform and warm up," Coach Clark said.

"But Coach, don't I have to try out for the team?" William asked. "Principal Schmidt said that tryouts already ended."

"I feel good about you," Coach Clark said. "I think we're going to beat Martland and win All-County for the first time in twenty years. I can taste it."

"But I'm telling you, Coach," William said plaintively, "I'm really not that good."

"Well-raised," the coach said, and he nodded and his large frame disappeared through the doorway.

"Well, I guess that's all settled," Principal Schmidt said, reaching out a hand to William. "Welcome to our school, son."

William looked at his mother and shrugged. She didn't know what to think.

"Let's get this party started!" William exclaimed. "Which way is my homeroom?"

"Not quite yet," said Principal Schmidt. "First I'd like you and your mother to meet your guidance counselor, Miss Newsome. I think you'll have a lot in common." He pointed out the door. "Follow the hallway all the way down, turn right, follow *that* hallway all the way down, and it's the first door on your left."

The Principal rose from his chair and smiled. "Ms. Barnes, let me just say again: we're very honored and excited to have your son in our school."

He seemed so sincere that Adele blushed.

"Thank you for making it so easy," she said, but to William she sounded more polite than convinced.

As they turned to leave the office, she winced as Principal Schmidt asked William, "So your friends really call you Lunch Money?"

Chapter 8

A FRIENDLY FACE

William and Adele found the door to the guidance counselor's office open. They peered inside, and to their amazement, they saw a young African-American woman on the phone. She was the first person of color they had seen since coming to Turnberry.

Adele and William stared at each other in surprise. Miss Newsome looked to be in her early thirties, light-skinned, with short, relaxed hair. She was on the phone, and she didn't sound happy.

"You're admitting him without any paperwork at all?" she was saying. "No transcripts, no vaccination record, no proof of residency, nothing? This is highly unusual, Principal Schmidt."

At that moment, the guidance counselor looked out into the hallway, where she saw Adele and William standing. Now she looked just as surprised as the two of them.

"I think they're here," she said into the phone. "I'll call you back."

She hung up, rose, and gave a knowing smile.

"You must be...*Lunch Money*?" she said tentatively, not sure if she was really supposed to call a student by a name like that.

"His name is William."

"But you can call me Lunch Money," William said, turning on the charm.

"William," the woman said with a sense of definiteness and even relief. "Please come in."

Adele and William entered her office.

"I'm Danielle Newsome," she said, extending a hand and a warm smile to Adele. "Welcome to our school."

"Adele Barnes," Adele said, studying Danielle, clasping her hand, and then taking a seat.

William also sat, looking expectantly at Danielle.

"You can imagine our surprise to see you," Adele said.

"We weren't sure black folk was even *allowed* in this town," William said, giving a friendly grin.

"William, mind your manners," Adele snapped.

"I'm just saying what you're thinking," William told his mother. And to Danielle: "Am I wrong?"

She gave a light shrug.

"I think the three of us," she began, choosing her words carefully, "are the only three African-Americans in a three-mile radius."

"I know what a radius is," William volunteered. "I just didn't know that radiuses didn't have any black people in them."

"Not this one," Danielle agreed. "So I hear you're coming to our school, William. Is that correct?"

"If they'll have me," he said.

Danielle gave a look of surprise. "Oh, they want you here," she said. "They want you bad."

"Because they think I can play basketball?" William said.

"Beats me," Danielle said. "But I've been here for four years, since they opened the school, and they've never admitted a student without all of the paperwork. They're real sticklers."

"What's this all about?" Adele asked. "I mean, I'm grateful the boy doesn't have to waste any time and that he can start right away, but what's the rush? Why the special treatment?"

"You heard the coach," William said disdainfully. "With me, they can beat Martland. Win that basketball trophy. With me, their shiny new point guard."

"Was that it?" Danielle asked, not quite believing it.

"The way the coach was looking at me," William said, "I was starting to think I was a nice, juicy T-bone steak, and he hadn't had a bite to eat for weeks."

"Is that true?" Danielle asked. "Not that I have any doubt, knowing Coach Clark."

"Is he a good guy?" Adele asked.

"He's fine," Danielle said. "So is Principal Schmidt. I guess they made certain assumptions."

"Like I can ball," William said. "Well, they're in for a rude awakening. Are they gonna throw me out of school when they find I can barely hit a J?"

Danielle laughed. "I don't think so," she said. "But they may remember they have a rule about paperwork."

"We can get all that together soon enough," Adele said. "Do you think I'm making a mistake? Bringing William here?"

Danielle shook her head.

"It's a great school," she said. "The faculty is terrific. The administration's pretty good. The parents are involved. The kids are nice. It's a great place to be."

"But what about for him?" Adele said. "I figured it would be mostly white, but I didn't expect—"

"That I'd stick out like a sore, black thumb," William said, finishing his mother's thought.

"That's not what I—" Adele began, and then she shook her head. "That's exactly what I meant."

Danielle thought for a moment before she replied. Adele and William were leaning forward intently, waiting to see how she would respond.

"We've had black families before," she said. "Not many. There were never any incidents. I just don't think they ever felt entirely...comfortable here."

The corners of Adele's mouth pulled downward into a small frown. "Are they going to accept William? That's all I'm concerned about."

Danielle nodded.

"There may be some awkward moments," she said, studying William to see if he could handle things here. "But nothing overt. These are decent people. They just haven't had that much contact with...."

Her voice trailed off.

"Actual, real-life black people," William said, finishing her sentence for her. "Except for you, of course."

Danielle grinned.

"I guess I'm representing," she said.

"And I guess I will, too," William said. "It's better than getting shaken down for my Lunch Money every day. And the two boys I met last night were okay. Red and Tommy."

Danielle nodded thoughtfully. "They're good kids," she said, reaching for a file folder. "Tommy's quite the little leader. And very smart. I'll put you in their homeroom."

"That would be great," Adele said, nodding gratefully.

"The only problem I have," William said slowly, "is that I'm really not that great an athlete. I'm decent, but Moms and Grandmama keep such an eye on me that I'm always home studying instead of out on the court. I'm just afraid that people are gonna be disappointed when they find I'm not the, you know, the great black hope."

Danielle nodded thoughtfully. "I'm sure they'll learn to like you for who you are," she assured William. "Not for who they think you are."

"That would be nice," William said.

"Your son will truly be in good hands here, Ms. Barnes," Danielle said. "I'll keep my eye out for him."

"That would be fantastic," Adele said. "Until I can get a transfer, I'll just be here on the weekends. The boy's grandmother will be taking care of him."

"That's fine," Danielle said. "I know that Principal Schmidt is making a big exception for William and letting him be admitted without the paperwork. But the sooner you can get all that stuff in, the better, if you know what I mean."

Adele nodded quickly.

"Well, Lunch--I mean, William—" Danielle began, blushing and looking at the clock radio on her desk, "you could still catch a few minutes of homeroom, if you want."

"Homeroom's my favorite subject," William said. "Right up there with lunch and recess. In fact, at my old school, I triple majored in those things."

Even Adele laughed.

"You'll do fine," Danielle said, rising, and William and Adele followed suit. "Let's get you to homeroom. And by the way, welcome to Turnberry Middle School. We're glad you're here."

William and Danielle shook hands.

"Thank you," William said, accepting the warm handshake. "But you can still call me Lunch Money. It's what I'm used to."

"His name is William," Adele said, quietly but firmly.

Danielle smiled.

Adele checked her watch. "I'm late enough for work as it is," she said uneasily. "I've got to get going. William, listen to the teachers and behave."

"Don't sweat it, Moms," William said, giving her a kiss. "I'll be fine."

"Thank you, Danielle," Adele said. "I won't lie. It makes things easier knowing you're here."

Adele and Danielle shook hands, and Adele was off.

"Right this way," Danielle said, and she led the way out of her office and down the long, brightly lit hall.

William took a deep breath and followed Danielle. *White people,* he thought, *get ready, because here I come.*

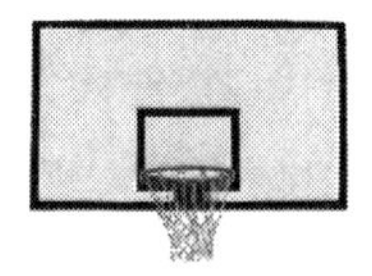

Chapter 9

HOMEROOM

"Hey, Lunch Money!"

William, following Danielle to his new homeroom, stopped suddenly in his tracks, amazed that anybody knew his nickname. He turned and saw Red coming back from the water fountain.

"Hey, Red," William said, reaching out to slap hands with him. An awkward moment ensued, because Red wasn't expecting to slap hands.

William made a mental note: *white people don't slap hands.*

Tommy emerged from the bathroom holding a hall pass. He gave William a friendly wave. "I see you got into our homeroom. Nice." He smiled at Miss Newsome. "We met Lunch Money last night. He's cool."

Cool in the sense of I've passed some sort of test? William wondered. *Or cool in the sense of, well, I'm cool?*

Either way, it was good.

"I'm glad you've already made some friends," Danielle said happily. "I've just got to say a word to Mr. Kenmore, but if you boys could take Lunch—I mean William—into the classroom, that would be great."

"Sure," Tommy and Red chorused.

They entered the classroom, where Mr. Kenmore, a tall, older, fit-looking white male with an almost military brush cut, was putting some notes on the board.

"Mr. Kenmore?" Danielle said, and he turned to see her standing with William, Tommy, and Red. "Sorry to interrupt."

"That's quite all right, Danielle," Mr. Kenmore said, studying William.

William wondered why she called him Mister, but he called her by her first name. He sighed. *Probably because he's white and she's black*, he thought. *Even here, the lines are in place.*

"This is William Barnes," she said. "He's coming into your homeroom, starting today."

Mr. Kenmore nodded and studied William. William, in turn, studied Mr. Kenmore—and the rest of the class. The students were so quiet you could have heard a pin drop. William had never walked into a classroom where not a single student was messing around with the teacher, cutting up or being rowdy. The teachers at his previous school had to work so hard to get the class's attention. But these were all well-mannered, well-scrubbed white kids, the girls' hair in plaits and neat ponytails, the boys in their button-down shirts and khakis, and they were all sitting ramrod straight in their chairs, giving Mr. Kenmore their undivided attention. It looked to Lunch Money like an advertisement for an uppity clothes store he might see in a glossy magazine, with one noticeable difference: they were all looking at him.

Like, *really* looking. He could feel a dozen sets of eyes boring into him.

"Welcome to our school," Mr. Kenmore said, extending a hand to William.

William correctly surmised that Mr. Kenmore wanted to shake his hand, not slap hands, and William gave him a nice, friendly handshake. "Happy to be here, sir," William said.

Mr. Kenmore smiled. "The only people who have to call me sir," he said, "are the Marines when I lead reserve duty. So you know these guys?" he added, indicating Tommy and Red.

William nodded. "We met last night."

"Great," Mr. Kenmore said, not really paying attention to William's answer. "Danielle, I assume he needs textbooks?"

"The works," she said. "I'll get a locker for him while he's in first period."

Mr. Kenmore nodded crisply. He turned back to his students. "Class, no talking. I'll be right back."

He looked at William. "Right this way, young man," he said, and led William to the supply closet at the back of the room.

A pretty girl with long blonde hair caught William's eye. She gave him a quizzical, "What are you doing here?" look that made William wince. What *was* he doing there? The same thing she was. Going to school. Trying to get an education. What was so strange about that?

William turned his attention back to Mr. Kenmore, who was peering into the darkness of the supply closet and pulled out a math textbook, a math workbook, a social studies textbook, an English workbook, and a Spanish text. William almost struggled under the weight of all the textbooks. He definitely wasn't expecting anything like that.

"You can keep them on my desk until you get a locker," Mr. Kenmore said. "You'll have math first period, right here in this room with me. So just keep the math textbook and workbook. After you get your locker, you can come collect the rest."

William nodded, but he was barely paying attention. He couldn't get over the textbooks.

They were all new.

Every single one of them.

The covers weren't torn off.

The pages weren't ripped or written on. There were nobody else's names on the books.

There wasn't any scribble-scrabble all over the sides, top, or bottom of any of the books. They were all completely *new*. And so shiny he could see his face in their reflection.

William had never seen a new textbook before in his life.

He heard someone giggle. He looked up to see the blonde girl from before, who had clamped her hand over her mouth, stifling another giggle. William couldn't decide if her laughter was mean-spirited, but he decided it wasn't. He knew he must have looked pretty ridiculous, standing there with his eyes bugging out at all those shiny new books.

He peered into the supply closet, and as his eyes adjusted to the darkness of the closet, he realized it was stacked with equally new, untouched textbooks.

He couldn't get over it.

"How much is all this?" he asked Mr. Kenmore, afraid his mother couldn't afford it.

Mr. Kenmore gave him a surprised look.

"It's free," he said, trying to gauge whether William was making fun of him. Mr. Kenmore realized William wasn't.

"Standard issue," he added. "Every student here gets exactly what you got."

"Why don't students at my old school get textbooks like these?" William heard himself asking, and then instantly regretted the question.

"Above my pay grade," Mr. Kenmore said. "The seat next to Tommy is free. You can sit there."

William nodded and handed over all his non-math textbooks to Mr. Kenmore, who took them and carried them to the front of the room and put them on his desk.

"Mm, mm, mm," William marveled. "These are the nicest textbooks I've ever seen."

"What kind of school did you go to?" Tommy asked. "What did they, like, burn books?"

"A poor school," William said. "My school was so poor, we couldn't pay attention."

Red and Tommy laughed, although William didn't think it was that funny.

William felt the heat of a dozen stares. He craned his neck to look around him, but as soon as he did, all eyes went back to their textbooks, or their desks, or fidgeting with their phones. *Wow*, William thought. *Look at all those smartphones!* Even though his Moms worked at the phone company and could get him a smartphone for free, his Grandmama would only let him have an old-fashioned flip phone with no Internet, and all it could do was make calls and text. Even in his old neighborhood he was the only kid without a smartphone. But when William complained about how uncool this made him, and why couldn't he just have a smartphone like all the other kids?, his Grandmama would shrug and say, "Ask the pastor."

A few girls in the back row of the classroom were whispering dramatically, and—judging by the way they kept glancing at William and tossing their hair—they were most definitely talking about him.

"Guess they've never seen someone as handsome as me," he told Tommy and Red, feeling self-conscious.

"It's just 'cause you're the new kid," Tommy assured him. "It's not because you're African-American."

"Probably so," William said, nodding vigorously, as if he believed it.

He thought about everything that had happened since he had entered the school building – the principal and the coach getting so excited because they thought he could ball. The office people staring at him like he was someone from another planet. Everyone was nice, but he still wondered what they were really thinking. He wondered whether he was better off with the hoodlums who took his Lunch Money. At least with people like that, he knew where he stood.

"Quiet, please," said Mr. Kenmore, and instantly the girls stopped whispering. "Students, we'd like to welcome a new member of our homeroom in sixth grade here at Turnberry Middle School. William Barnes is just joining us. I hope you'll all join me in making him feel welcome."

The students burst into prolonged applause.

William, embarrassed by the attention, gave a self-conscious smile and waved.

"It's got to be a little overwhelming for Mr. Barnes," Mr. Kenmore continued. "So do everything you can to make him feel at ease."

"He likes to be called Lunch Money," Tommy said, and the students all looked at him to see if he was telling the truth.

"You can call me Lunch Money," William said, trying to sound friendly.

In fact, he was a little bit scared. He had never seen so many white people in one place in his life. It wasn't that he had a problem with that—he didn't—it was more that he wasn't sure how they expected him to behave. He got the sense they were all waiting for him to *say* or *do* something, maybe to crack wise like the black characters they'd seen in TV shows or on the silver screen, and he didn't want to disappoint them.

A student's voice crackled over the P.A. system, startling William, though no one else in the classroom seemed surprised. "I know I've already made the announcements this morning," said the voice excitedly, "though in case you zoned out, here's a brief recap..." The student quickly and spiritedly went over the lunch menu in the cafeteria, science fair, and a PTA project to raise money for solar panels for the school. Then, to William's surprise and embarrassment, he heard his own name mentioned.

"But the real reason for this second string of announcements is that we want to welcome our newest student, William Barnes. William will be point guard for the Turnberry Titans, and Coach Clark says that this is the year we finally beat Martland for the county championship."

"Oh," William said, and he gave an uneasy smile as his fellow students studied him with a new measure of curiosity.

"You made the team," Tommy said, offering William a fist bump, which he returned. Then he leaned in closer. "Um, no offense, buddy, but…have they actually seen you play basketball?"

William grimaced. "Nope. And don't worry—no offense taken. I can't help but think this is not going to end well."

The bell rang, signaling the end of homeroom. William's educational career at Turnberry Middle School had officially begun.

Chapter 10

LUNCH MONEY EATS LUNCH (FINALLY)

I've got to warn you," Red said. "The food here stinks."

William had completed his first morning of classes at his new school, and each successive class followed the same pattern.

First, William could not get over how well behaved his classmates were. When the bell rang, they were already in their seats. In each class, all of the kids—not just a few in the front—had their binders, textbooks, and workbooks open to the right page.

They were ready to learn, all of them.

No one was sleeping.

There were no empty seats.

The students were consistently respectful toward the teachers.

There had been only one behavioral incident the whole day, when a kid was busted for texting during class. He willingly gave up his phone without threatening the life of the teacher. That was a new one for William.

And now it was lunchtime, and the money Adele had given William for lunch was still sitting securely in the pocket of his freshly pressed jeans. No one had even glanced at him in such a way to make him think that he would have to give it up.

"It's bad, huh?" William asked, as he, Tommy, and Red entered the cafeteria, grabbed trays, and headed for the food line.

"The worst," Red said, shaking his head.

"The food was pretty bad at my old school," William said. "I guess here it must be *really* terrible."

It made sense, in a way, William reasoned. If the school spent all their money on fresh paint for the building, and school desks and chairs that didn't look 100 years old, and stacks of brand-new textbooks, not to mention nylon nets for the basketball hoops, and who knows what all else sporting equipment, no wonder they had to skimp on lunch.

It sure *smelled* good, though.

The only thing that bothered William about his experience in school to that moment was the fact that whenever his teachers spoke directly to him, they spoke a little more slowly and a little more loudly than they did to the rest of the kids.

As if William couldn't hear them.

Or as if he were from another country and didn't speak English.

Or as if he were stupid.

Well, William thought, as he inspected the options for lunch—spaghetti and meatballs or fried chicken—he might not be first in his class, but he wouldn't be the most stupid kid, either. He was prepared to work twice as hard, just as his Grandmama had said the night before. Whatever it took.

I like it here, he told himself. *I'm going to make this work.*

The serving lady looked at him with curiosity, either because he was new or because he was black. *Or both*, William thought. He sighed. *Might as well get used to it.*

"Spaghetti and meatballs, please," he said.

"The fried chicken's good, too," the cafeteria lady said.

William stopped and thought for a moment.

Was she recommending the fried chicken because...then he just shook his head. It was wearying trying to filter every conversation through the lens of race. If they weren't used to black people here, they'd have to get used to us. Or at least to me.

"No thanks," William said. "I'll just stick with the spaghetti and meatballs."

The cafeteria lady dolloped a large portion of spaghetti and meatballs on William's plate.

"Vegetable special?" she asked, her serving tool poised dramatically above the carrots and green beans.

"Yes, please," William said enthusiastically.

"Lunch Money, you like vegetables?" Tommy asked disdainfully.

"Sure," he said. "My Grandmama has a huge garden behind our house. Our old house, that is. I guess she'll start a new garden here."

To William's amazement, when the cafeteria lady pushed his plate on the counter toward him, the vegetables looked just as fresh as his grandmother's.

He had never seen fresh vegetables in school before.

Must be the spaghetti and meatballs are so terrible, he decided. Although they didn't look that bad.

William headed down the cafeteria line behind Tommy and Red, grabbed a container of chocolate milk and a small package of cookies, and paid for his food.

It cost exactly half of what lunch cost at his old school.

Not that he'd gotten to taste that very often.

And it looked ten times better.

"Thank you," William said as he took back all the unexpected change. "I feel rich!"

He followed the boys to an empty table in the crowded cafeteria. The other boys dug into their food. William closed his eyes, bowed his head, and said a quick grace, at first hoping the other kids wouldn't notice, and then deciding that it didn't matter if they did. His Grandmama had taught him to say grace for any meal. He wasn't about to stop now, just because he was the only African-American in a sea of white faces.

He bit into the spaghetti and meatballs, expecting the worst.

To his surprise, it was delicious.

It was beyond delicious. He couldn't *believe* how good it was.

"This is unbelievable!" he exclaimed.

Red gave him a sympathetic nod. "We told you it was bad," he said, embarrassed for his school.

"I like it," William admitted, taking another huge bite. "Best school food I ever ate."

He thought for a moment about all the times that those hoodlums had taken his Lunch Money.

"Practically the *only* school food I ever ate," he added.

"You like it?" Tommy asked, surprised.

"What's not to like?" William replied, through a mouthful of food. "Can you get seconds?"

"Only if you don't mind having a stomach operation," Tommy said. "There ought to be a law."

"There ought to be a law against the food at my *old* school," William said. "Or did I just get lucky with this one meal? Maybe everything else stinks. Is that right?"

Tommy and Red looked at each other.

"If you can stand the spaghetti and meatballs," Tommy reasoned, "you'll probably like everything."

"Are you psyched about basketball practice this afternoon?" Red asked.

The change in subject came as a relief to William, who was feeling embarrassed about how much he liked the food.

"I guess," William said. "I just feel like the expectations they're putting on me are pretty big. I mean, why did they have to go and announce that whole thing on the P.A. system?"

"They're just excited," Tommy said.

William shrugged.

"They shouldn't get excited 'til they see me actually play," he said.

Tommy nodded. "Anyway, we already have a point guard," he said. "Martin. I told you about him last night. He's been a point guard since he was seven years old. He's probably not too happy that Coach gave away his position."

"He can have it back," William said, through a mouthful of spaghetti. "I never said I was point guard material."

"Here he comes," Tommy said, nodding at a tall, athletic, mean-looking kid who had just paid for his plate of food: a steaming pile of spaghetti—twice the portion size everyone else had gotten—and a tall plastic glass of orange juice.

"Martin," Tommy called out, "sit with us."

Martin came by. Even though he was still in the sixth grade, he was just a few inches shy of six feet tall. *Point guard?* William thought. *He ought to be jumping center.*

"Not with him," Martin said, nodding coolly at William.

He was evidently angry about William taking his position on the team. He was so controlled about his anger, so poised, that he looked even scarier.

"I don't know who thinks you ought to be point guard," Martin said menacingly, trying to stare William down.

"*I* certainly don't think I should be point guard," William replied.

Martin cocked his head and studied him.

"You making fun of me?" he asked, and he somehow sounded even taller and more menacing than before.

"I'm not making fun of anything," William said. "I'm just telling you what I'm telling myself. I'm not that good. I keep saying it, but nobody seems to listen."

"We'll see how good you are at practice," Martin said, glowering at William. "You better bring your A-game, punk."

"Chill out," Red said hotly. "It's Lunch Money's first day. Give him a break."

Martin grinned. William thought Martin had teeth the size of a large dog's.

"You don't get to tell me to chill out," Martin said. "If you want to be point guard, Mr. Lunch Money, you're going to have to take it away from me."

"The coach already gave it to him!" Tommy exclaimed. "Will you knock it off?"

"Shut your mouth, O'Connell," Martin said. "Or I'll shut it for you. And your mouth is the only thing you got going for you."

At that moment, Coach Clark, who had been on cafeteria duty, stepped over.

"Looks like it's getting a little heated here, fellas," he said. "Martin, have you met your new teammate?"

"I met him." Martin scowled. "But I don't like him. And I don't have to like him."

"Just try to be friendly," Coach said. "Save your animosity for Martland."

Martin stomped off, still clutching his tray, and for a moment William worried about the guy's OJ sloshing all over his spaghetti. *That wouldn't taste very good.*

"Don't worry about Martin," Coach Clark said. "It's not about race. He's an equal opportunity hater."

"I didn't take it personally," William said, surprised that the coach even mentioned race. "I'm sure he's a good guy when you get to know him."

"Not really," Tommy and Red chorused.

"Be at the gym at three," Coach Clark said. "You'll get your uniform then. I like your style, Barnes."

And with that, the coach walked away to settle a dispute at another table.

"All that arguing made me even hungrier," Lunch Money said, rising to his feet. "I'm gonna get me more spaghetti and meatballs. Even try the fried chicken. Anybody want anything else?"

The boys both shook their heads. Lunch Money headed toward the food line, ready to reload.

Chapter 11

BALLIN'

The afternoon went as smoothly for William as had his morning, minus the slight hiccup with Martin the Angry Giant. But once again, his teachers spoke a little more slowly and a little more loudly to him than to the other students, which William felt somewhat insulting and patronizing. At one point, he nearly raised his hand and said, "I've lived in the United States all my life and I understand English pretty well. And my hearing is perfect, so you don't have to raise your voice, and you don't have to slow down. I'm tracking with what you're saying."

William didn't do it because he didn't want to embarrass himself, and in some sense he felt he was something of an ambassador on behalf of African-Americans everywhere. He figured anything he did or said would be used as a weapon against all black people.

Suddenly he felt a new respect for those Civil Rights luminaries whose portraits graced the walls of his home, both here in Turnberry and back in the city. Nobody was exactly on his case or bothering him. In fact, people couldn't have been nicer. But still, he felt like he was being treated as "The Other" in strange, subtle, smiling ways. He felt a deeper bond with the leaders of the Civil Rights movement than ever before.

His first school day in Turnberry finally ended, at 2:40 pm, in P.E., in a gym that was as big and pretty as anything he had seen watching the NBA on TV. Not exactly, but it was still a million times nicer than the smelly old gym in his old school, which looked as though it had seen better days a few generations of students before William got there. The floor of the Turnberry Middle School gym practically glistened. It was so clean, William thought he could eat off it. Nylon nets fluttered from the basketball hoops, inviting shot after shot. Of course, the kids were playing volleyball, which William had never seen before, instead of basketball. But he knew he'd be playing basketball soon enough.

When the last bell rang, Tommy and Red led William to the boys' locker room, which had actual working showers. For a minute, William wondered if he had died and gone to middle school heaven. The lockers looked shiny and new. No graffiti anywhere. And then came the most amazing moment of all.

Coach Clark called William into his office, which wasn't that much—it might have been a converted closet with a lot of exposed cinderblock. It was only half the size of Danielle's office, William noted with a perverse sense of pride. She might not have been the coach, and everybody knows the coach is the most important person on the faculty of any school, but at least she had a window.

"All right, young man," Coach Clark said. "What are you, about five-one? Why don't you try on this uniform right here."

The coach nodded at a table that was actually an old door propped up on wooden stilts. The setting wasn't much, but what lay on it was the most exquisite thing William had ever seen. It was a powder blue basketball uniform, brand new, looking as if it had never even been in the washing machine. William just stared at it, afraid to touch it, thinking that if he did touch it, suddenly the whole thing might turn into a dream, and he'd be back in his own bed in his Grandmama's house in the city, having to get up and walk to school and give up his Lunch Money to those bullies, like always.

But it was no dream. He touched the uniform, and it felt soft and luxurious, like a king's robes in some cartoon adventure movie. He traced his fingers over the white script that said "Turnberry" on the front of the jersey. Some seamstress in some far-off land had labored at a sewing machine to create this uniform...this perfect stitching...just for him.

It was way too much to believe.

Coach Clark laughed, shattering the moment.

"Pick it up," he said. "It won't bite."

"Can't be sure," William murmured. He gave the coach a sidelong glance and then he noticed that Tommy and Red were standing at the entrance to the coach's office, already wearing their perfect, powder-blue uniforms, which they probably took for granted. No doubt.

William thought for a moment, held his breath, and picked up the uniform—the shirt and the jersey. To his astonishment, there were even matching socks—long, white tube socks that also looked as if they had never been worn. "This is all for me?" he asked the coach in disbelief. "Like, I'm supposed to wear this?"

"Unless you want to play in jeans and a t-shirt," Coach Clark said, slowly realizing that William had never seen anything this nice, up close, in his life.

"If you don't put it on, you're going to be late for practice," Coach Clark admonished him.

Fear of being late pushed William into action. He grabbed the uniform shorts and socks, nodded a quick thanks, and headed back into the locker room to change.

He caught sight of himself in a full-length mirror—a full-length mirror!—outside the boys' room.

Whoa, William thought. *I look fine.*

But then he was gripped with fear. These people expected him, for obvious reasons, to save their basketball team. Nobody, from the principal to the coach to the teachers and maybe even to the guidance counselor, Danielle, believed him when he said he lacked skills. His heart sank.

It's one thing for teachers to think I'm stupid. I have every chance of proving them wrong once I start turning in homework and taking tests. But on the basketball court? I'll be exposed. There's no place I can hide.

William gave serious thought to going back into the locker room, peeling off the uniform, thanking the coach, and then running all the way back to his new home, but he quickly thought better of it. Maybe they would take away his admission, especially because he didn't have any papers filed. He knew that made no sense. He knew his admission wasn't contingent on his ability to play. But somehow, his self-respect was. Or at least the image that he was expected to present.

"I'm really not any good," William said to no one in particular. And then he trotted out toward the basketball court, with all the enthusiasm of a man being led to his own execution.

All of a sudden he felt a ball shoved into his chest.

It was Martin.

"What's the big idea?" William asked, as soon as he could draw breath again.

Martin sneered at him.

"This is my house," Martin said. "And I'm the point guard on this team. If you think you're gonna take my job, you're wrong. And I don't care if you're black, white, red, or green. You're going *down*."

By now, all the other boys on the team had stopped whatever they were doing—stretching, shooting baskets, or practicing passing—and had circled around Martin and William.

William looked around at the circle of white faces.

He consoled himself with the thought that none of them had switchblades. He knew this was true because none of them had pockets. He checked their socks, just to be sure. He turned toward Martin.

"If you're gonna trash talk," William began, sounding more courageous than he felt, "you better have something interesting to say. So far, everything you say just makes me yawn."

"Oh, yeah?" Martin exclaimed, and he looked like he wanted to kill William, or at least scare him out of the building and back down the street to his mama. But William was having none of it. His Grandmama's words echoed through his mind: *If you don't stand up for yourself the first time, you'll fall for anything over and over.*

"I'll show you how to talk trash," he said, gathering his courage. "Yo mama so fat, when she backs up, you can hear beep, beep, beep."

The other kids burst into shocked laughter.

Martin spluttered but could not make a response.

"Yo mama so ugly," William continued, "they only keep negatives of her picture in the family album."

Martin dropped his jaw as if he were trying to say something, but no words came out.

"Yo mama so dumb," William said, warming to the subject, "she couldn't spell cat if you spotted her the C and the A."

The boys hooted and hollered when they heard that one. All of a sudden, Coach Clark appeared.

"What's going on?" he demanded, seeing the boys circled around Martin and William.

"We're just having a friendly conversation," William chirped. "You know, like the song." Then he started to sing: "Getting to know you...getting to know all about you..."

Everyone cracked up, except Martin, who looked even angrier than before, if such a thing were possible. Even the coach was trying hard to suppress a smile.

"That's what we need around here if we're going to beat Martland," Coach Clark said happily. "A little attitude. Okay, pair off. Layup drills."

The boys paired off, Martin slowly stepping away from William, giving him one last glare before finding another boy with whom to practice. Red tapped William on the shoulder and they paired off and began the layup drill.

"You better be careful, dude," Red said. "Martin's the school bully."

"I've seen worse," William said, thinking back to some of the guys he had seen on basketball courts in his neighborhood. "He don't scare me."

"He scares me," Red said. "He scares me a lot."

"Whatever," William said, and he took and made his first layup.

"Got that out of the way," he said, relieved.

"Courtesy," Red said, bounce-passing William the ball. "Did you stay up all night practicing or something? Last night you said you stank."

"I stink up the gym," William said matter-of-factly as he went in for another easy layup. He made that one, too.

"If you say so," Red said. "But seriously—what the heck happened between yesterday and today?"

"Beginner's luck," William said as he made his third layup. "That's my story and I'm sticking to it."

"Do you think I'll ever get to shoot today?" Red said, grinning and then passing William the ball.

"Any minute now," William said, and this time he went up, changed hands in midair, and sank a layup left-handed, the ball bouncing off his shoulder as he returned to earth. "My lucky streak's probably gonna end right now."

But it didn't. By the time the coach blew his whistle to end the layup drill, William had made fifteen straight shots. Red had done nothing but rebound the ball. He hadn't gotten to shoot once.

"Passing drill," Coach Clark said, and the boys went into a passing routine that William observed and quickly picked up. The coach had been watching his layups. Now he watched William pass the ball with precision to teammate after teammate.

Five minutes later, Coach Clark blew his whistle again. "Foul shots," he ordered, and the team lined up at three different baskets to shoot fouls.

William couldn't understand it. Everything he chucked at the basket went in. *Everything*. If he was off balance, the shot went in. If it hit the backboard, even when he intended to hit nothing but net, it went in. Bank shots went in. Left-handed shots went in. Hook shots went in. *Everything* went in. Maybe the shots rattled around for a little while, but eventually, *boom*. Two points. Or three points, because his shooting was just as solid when Coach Clark changed the drill to shooting three-pointers. William finally missed a few, but that was because he was shooting with his eyes closed.

"I thought you told me you had no game," Coach Clark said to William, putting his arm around the boy's shoulders.

"I know you think I'm all that and a bag of chips," William said, catching his breath, "but I just got lucky."

"Forty-six out of fifty is lucky?" Coach Clark replied, incredulous. "You're a sharpshooter. You're a gunner. I can't waste talent like yours at point guard. You're our new power forward. Let's all give it up for Lunch Money."

The other kids hooted and hollered. At least, all of them except Martin.

"What are you so upset about?" William asked Martin. "You get to keep your job."

"I'm the star of this team," Martin told William, stepping within a foot and a half of William's face. "I don't care *what* position you play. Just make sure you understand that."

"And I got crazy lucky today," William said. "I shot out of my mind. I'm not that good. I hope you understand."

Martin didn't know what to make of that comment, because there was nothing trash talk-ish about it. Martin glowered at him and headed for the locker room.

Tommy put his arm around William.

"I had no idea you were that good," Tommy said. "I mean, no offense, but you *weren't* that good when we played H-O-R-S-E last night. Were you holding out on us?"

"I wasn't. Honest." William scratched his head. "I don't know what happened just now."

"Whatever happened," Tommy said, "was awesome. You should make it happen again. You were off the chain."

William grinned. The compliment meant a lot to him. It also sounded funny to hear an expression he associated with his old neighborhood coming out of the mouth of a kid with splotchy brown freckles and an impressive vocabulary.

"You want to come over to my house this afternoon?" Tommy asked. "I've got Kanye's new CD. The guy's a poet—the Tupac of our age."

"Maybe after I do my homework," William said, happy with the invitation. "Catch you later."

The boys exchanged fist bumps. William went to his locker, collected his clothing, and looked around for Martin. No sign. He had ducked out while William was still talking with his friends. William felt like wearing his uniform home. He couldn't wait to put it in the washer and get it super clean for tomorrow's practice.

He grabbed his schoolbooks out of the gym locker and walked the two blocks to the house where they were staying. He wasn't even sure if he was going in the right direction until he saw his grandmother sitting out on the porch waiting for him.

He wondered what a white family would think if suddenly there was an African-American kid in a basketball uniform standing on their doorstep. They'd probably think I was raising money for the team, William decided. To pay for the uniforms.

"How was school?" she asked, studying him for signs of, well, anything.

"It was good, Grandmama," William said. "Except for one problem."

"What happened?" His grandmother asked, her eyes narrowing. "They give you trouble because you're black?"

William shook his head. "No, it's the opposite," he said. "I'm in trouble because I shot the ball *too* well. They're gonna think I can do that every time. Hey, I'm hungry. Got anything cooking on the stove?"

"Only some chicken and rice," Beatrice said, slowly getting up out of her chair on the porch. "I hope they didn't steal your Lunch Money."

"Nah," William exclaimed, reaching into his pocket and taking out two one-dollar bills and some coins. "I've even got change!"

"Mm, mm, mm," Beatrice said, and she followed William into the house.

Chapter 12

MILK AND COOKIES

"How was school?" Adele asked, as Beatrice and William went inside their house.

"School was fine," William said, surprised to see his mother. "I thought you were going back to work."

He put his textbooks carefully on the dining room table. He didn't fling them, as he did in his previous home, because they were so new and valuable.

"I took the day off," Adele said, studying him to see how the day went. "I was working on getting your paperwork together. How's my baby?"

"Your baby is fine." William grinned, reassuring her. "You look like you were waiting for a real baby to arrive, not just me coming home from school."

"Hungry?" Beatrice offered.

William thought before he spoke.

"Not overly," he said. "Maybe a little snack."

"Are you feeling well?" Adele asked, stepping forward to feel his forehead.

"What did they do to you?" Beatrice asked, equally concerned.

William gently removed his mother's hand from his forehead.

"They didn't do anything to me," he said. "Including taking my Lunch Money. I think that's why I'm not hungry. I've never known what it's like to eat a school lunch! By the way, the food there is awesome. Not as good as yours, Grandmama, but a million times better than my old school!"

Adele looked relieved.

"I'll get you some milk and cookies," Beatrice said, feeling the need to feed William *something*. She bustled off to the kitchen. William couldn't believe it. Since when had his grandmother let him eat dessert first? Usually when he asked for a cookie or ice cream before dinner, Grandmama laughed and said, "Ask the pastor!"—and the conversation ended right then and there.

Adele and William sat down at the dining room table.

"How was it?" she asked cautiously.

"It was…*amazing*," William said. "It was...like a spa. Not that I've ever been to a spa. But if I ever go, I wouldn't be surprised if it's just like this school."

"Were the people nice?" Adele asked, still studying him carefully. "That's a lovely uniform."

"I'm telling you, Moms," William said. "This school is awesome. I never want to leave."

"Did they...treat you differently?"

William thought about the teachers who spoke slowly and loudly.

"A little bit," he said, "but that might've been because I'm new."

Adele gave him a concerned look.

William looked resigned. "Okay," he admitted. "We know why they treated me differently. But they didn't treat me *badly*. And I think they'll get used to me. I think they might even be happy to have me there. I can tell you Coach Clark was!"

"How was practice?" she asked.

"There's one kid who doesn't like me," William said. "But I know it's not because I'm African-American. It's because he was going to be point guard. But he still is. So no harm, no foul."

"What are you talking about?" Adele said, confused.

"It'll take too long to explain," William assured her, touching her wrist. "Moms, it's all good. Truly."

Adele took a moment to absorb the good news. The relief etched into her expression was palpable.

"I was so worried," she admitted. "All day long, I thought, I overreacted. I did a dumb thing. But what you're saying is, this can work."

William nodded vigorously. "I don't want to leave," he said. "I like this place. The kids are a little strange, but in a good way."

Adele looked puzzled.

"First," William began, "they all sit nicely in class. They're not lounged all over the chairs like they're in some club and the teacher's just there to provide bottle service."

"What do you know about bottle service?" Adele asked, bothered by William's apparent sophistication.

William blushed. "Actually, I don't know what that means," he admitted. "But all the kids in my school—my old school—would talk about getting bottle service at clubs. It just sounds good."

"It's not for you," Adele said firmly. "Go on."

"When the bell rings?" William asked, his voice rising into a question. "All the kids are just sitting nicely. Their books are open. To the right page, even. Nobody's snoring in the back, sleeping off a hangover or whatever. It's like they actually came to school to learn something."

Adele nodded, taking it all in.

"What did *you* learn?" she asked, her tone firm but not unkind.

"Oh, I learned something all right," William said, nodding firmly. "I learned we *poor*."

Adele looked sharply at him. "What are you talking about?"

"Look at this uniform!" William exclaimed, grabbing it by the shoulder band as Beatrice put a plate of cookies and a glass of milk in front of him and sat down opposite Adele. "Ain't nobody ever worn it before me!"

"*No one* ever wore it before me," Beatrice corrected him.

William rolled his eyes.

"If I can't be black in my own house," he said to Beatrice, "where *can* I be?"

"Being black doesn't mean sounding ignorant," Beatrice rebuked.

"Whatever," William said, rolling his eyes. "But seriously. Look at this uniform! It looks like it just came out of the NBA store! And look at my schoolbooks! They're all brand-new. They had a whole big closet of books ain't nobody even touched!"

Beatrice rapped her knuckles on the table.

"*That no one has ever touched*," William said sarcastically. "The gym looks like the Staples Center. All the classrooms have fresh paint. The desks are shiny and new. Ain't no—there's no carving of initials or curse words in the desks or chairs. It's all showroom fresh."

Adele just shook her head.

"How come," William asked, "white kids get all the nice stuff and black kids get all the crappy stuff?"

Adele pursed her lips and paused, thinking through how best to answer the question.

"It's complicated," she said. "The real answer is that school districts get their money from taxes. People in a community like this pay a lot more in taxes than they do where we live. So the schools have more money here. Does that make sense?"

"It makes *logic*," William said thoughtfully, "but it doesn't make *sense*."

Adele looked compassionately at her son. "I know what you mean," she said.

"The kids were nice," William said. "Especially Red and Tommy. It's like they were looking out for me today, because I was new. Not because I was black. Because I was new. That was the sense I got."

Adele looked skeptical. "I hope you're right," she said, not sounding convinced.

"I don't want to go back to my old school," William said. "I'd rather be the black kid here than another poor kid there."

"We're not poor," Adele said, eyes flashing. "We own our own home. I work. We have our dignity."

"Well, maybe I don't want to live around people who don't," William said. Then he grinned. "Maybe there's a white kid inside me trying to escape. Maybe I was supposed to be born white."

Beatrice shook her head. "Hush your mouth," she said disdainfully.

"I'm just joshing," William said. "I'm proud to be who I am and what I am. You know that. But the thing is, why go to school? To get an education. I think I can get a much better education here. Hands down. I think the teachers think I might be stupid, but they'll find out I'm not. So I'm not worried about that."

Adele studied him.

"So what *are* you worried about?" she asked.

William frowned.

"Basketball," he said.

"I thought you said the coach liked you," Adele said, sounding confused.

"That's the *problem*," William said, suddenly serious. "He likes me too much. I shot the lights out in practice today."

Both Adele and Beatrice looked confused.

"I shot really well," William explained. "I made almost every shot I took. I was shooting threes with my eyes closed and making almost all of them. It was sick."

"What's sick about making shots?" Beatrice asked, confused. "Isn't that the whole point?"

"It's like there was some little space creature sitting on the rim," William said, at a loss for any other explanation, "just making sure every shot I took went in. The only problem is, it's like I told Principal Schmidt and Coach Clark first thing this morning. *I'm not that good.* I had a lucky half hour in the gym. But they're all gonna think that I can do that every time."

Adele reached for one of William's cookies and took a thoughtful bite.

"Well, why can't you?" she asked.

William shook his head quickly.

"You don't understand," he said plaintively. "They're all gonna think that I can play that well all the time. And then when my game reverts to its usual level, which is pretty bad, they're all gonna think I'm doggin' it. Trying to make the team look bad. This is the only thing. It's not gonna end well. I don't even want to be on the team."

"So tell the coach," Adele said. "Tell the principal."

"The only black kid in school doesn't want to play basketball?" William asked. "That's just gonna make me look weird."

"But that's just reinforcing a prejudice they have," Adele said.

"I'm a sixth grader," William said. "I'm not a race man," and he nodded at the portraits of the Civil Rights leaders.

Adele finished the cookie.

"I understand," she said, rubbing his shoulder. "That uni does feel nice. They just gave that to you?"

"Let me wear it out of the building," William said. "I guess if I don't go to school tomorrow, the repo man will show up at our door. 'Bam! Bam! Bam! Where's that uniform? I'm here to pick up that uniform!'"

"That's not even funny," Adele said, trying not to laugh.

"All right, Moms," William said. "I better get my studying done. If I'm gonna represent the entire African-American community tomorrow in math class, I better know how to measure the area of a rectangle."

"The basketball thing will work itself out," Adele said, as she rose to give William some privacy so he could get his homework done.

William frowned again. "I hope so," he said. "But I'm just not sure."

Chapter 13

DOGGING IT?

After dinner, as William was washing and drying the dishes—only children have nowhere to hide when it comes to chores—the doorbell rang.

Beatrice was reading Scripture and Adele was on her laptop at the dining room table, trying to make up for the day's work she had missed. William dried his hands and went to the door.

It was Tommy and Red. Red was carrying a basketball.

"Lunch Money," Tommy said. "Shoot some hoops?"

William shot a glance at his mother, who grimaced at the mention of her son's nickname, but gave a quick nod.

"Home by dark," she said.

"You got it, Moms," William said.

Happily, he headed out the door with his new friends.

"So," Tommy said as they walked to the schoolyard. "How do you like our school?"

"I like it fine," William replied. "Best school I've ever seen."

"Cool," Red said, bouncing the ball on the sidewalk.

"It's just okay," Tommy said. "I mean, it's not inferior, but it's not superior, either."

William raised an eyebrow.

"Just okay?" he asked. "You don't care for it?"

Tommy made a face. "I don't know," he said. "Half of the classes are boring. Maybe all of them. I don't feel intellectually... challenged."

"At least you've got good textbooks," William said.

Tommy actually laughed.

"Are you kidding me?" he asked, studying William to see if William was making fun of him. "Our textbooks are the most boring I've ever seen in my life. Don't tell me you like them."

William shrugged. He didn't know what to say. So he figured he would just tell the truth.

"At my old school," he said, "our textbooks were all raggedy. The covers were knocked off. There was scribble-scrabble all over them. You could hardly read what they said."

"Just because they're new doesn't mean they're any good," Tommy countered. "The stuff in those books—it doesn't make you think outside the box. It's just about memorizing a bunch of boring facts."

"What he's saying is," Red said, "we thought you were a jock, not a nerd."

"Can't you be both?" William asked. "I mean, do you have to be one or the other?"

Tommy and Red glanced at each other. They had no idea.

"Most people around here are kind of one or the other," Tommy finally said, passing the ball to William. "But you're right: maybe that's just another way of being stuck inside the box."

"I don't think you realize how good your school is," William said frankly. "It's all brand new and shiny. I think it's just great."

"You think school is great?" Red asked, studying William as if he had come from Mars and not the city fifty miles away. "Nobody thinks school is great!"

"Well, I do," William said stubbornly. "You just don't have a basis of comparison."

"A what?" Red asked, confused.

Tommy sighed. "A basis of comparison, Red. Maybe you *should* be studying more."

They had reached the schoolyard. "See those nets?" William said. "Until yesterday, only place I'd ever seen nets? On TV."

"Huh," Red said, staring at the net as if he had never seen it before.

"And your school food?" William continued. "At my school, we call hamburgers murderburgers because they taste like the cafeteria ladies are trying to kill you."

Both boys laughed.

"I've never seen anyone as excited by food as you were by the spaghetti and meatballs today," Tommy said. "It's like you'd found the Ark of the Covenant."

"It's not like I got to eat the food at my old school all that often," William allowed, as Red passed him the ball. "You know why everybody calls me Lunch Money."

"Actually, we don't," Red said.

William felt himself blushing. "It's cause some of the kids used to take my Lunch Money, that's all," he admitted.

"That's wrong," said Red.

William looked quickly at him to see if he was teasing.

Red looked sincere. William settled down.

William tried a bank shot and missed. The ball clanged off the rim.

"Compared to my old school?" William continued. "The food here is like a five-star hotel."

Tommy and Red looked at each other.

William passed Tommy the ball.

"And I saved the best for last," William said, as Tommy drained a layup. "Those uniforms."

"Let me guess," Red said sarcastically. "You loooove the uniforms here."

William nodded as he chased down the rebound and passed it back to Red. "Do you know what it's like not to wear a uniform that's all caked with years of dried sweat? That's all frayed and the number's falling off? You guys just don't know how good you have it."

Tommy held the ball and didn't shoot.

"You might be right," he admitted. "I never thought about it that way."

"Me neither," Red said.

Tommy bounce-passed the ball to William, who threw up another brick.

"There's one thing we're really confused about," Red said as he grabbed the rebound and passed it back to William, who fired up an air ball.

"What's that?" William asked innocently.

"Who's the real Lunch Money?" Tommy asked, a slight edge to his voice.

William just stared at him, and Tommy stared back.

"Last night," Tommy said, "when we were out here shooting, you couldn't buy a basket. Same thing right now. But then when you got on the court with Coach and the whole team watching, you were lights out."

"You kept saying over and over," Red added, "'I can't shoot! I can't shoot!' Well, can you or can't you?"

William suddenly looked not just serious but scared.

"I've got no idea what happened in the gym today," he admitted. "I've never shot like that in my life. In my old neighborhood, when we chose up teams? I would get picked after the *white* kids."

William waited for the boys to laugh, but they didn't.

Oh, well, he thought. *Joke works for Chris Rock.*

"Seriously," he continued, "I'm not a baller. Everybody here thinks I am because I'm African-American. They even let me in school today without the paperwork, just so I could be at practice.

"I truly don't know what happened today. Maybe it was some kind of reverse nervousness. I knew how bad I was and figured I was just gonna stink up the gym. So instead, everything went in. But I don't expect that ever to happen again. And neither should anybody else."

Tommy and Red digested William's explanation.

Tommy didn't buy it.

"I just can't figure it out," he said. "I was thinking, were you setting us up last night by playing so badly? Because if you can shoot like that one time, you can shoot like that every time."

Red nodded. "Yeah, dude. No way what happened today was dumb luck."

William felt panic.

"You gotta believe me. I wouldn't lie about this. I can't ball. I got incredibly lucky today. Every dog has his day, and today was my day. But that's not gonna happen again.

"And I'm afraid when it doesn't, everybody's gonna look at me like, what's wrong with that black kid? I thought all black kids could ball! Why can't he?

"I mean, maybe they'll kick me out of school. Coach will kick me off the team for sure. I'm sorry I even came to practice."

"Then why'd you try out for the team?" Red asked, confused.

"I didn't try out for the team!" William said, his tone defensive. "It was all Principal Schmidt's idea. I was sitting there in his office this morning trying to get enrolled, and he called in Coach, and the two of them looked at me like I was some sort of juicy steak that could shoot the three.

"And now I got that kid Martin all mad at me because he thinks I'm gonna be point guard. I can't shoot. I can't pass. I can't ball. Now you guys don't even believe it."

Red and Tommy looked at each other.

"How many other black kids have you ever known?" William asked, his indignation rising. "You probably only saw black kids on TV! In sitcoms, or And One videos! Well, I'm here to break the news to you. Not all African-Americans are athletes. No matter what you see on TV. So just get over yourselves. I thought you guys were gonna be my friends."

"Lunch Money, dude, we didn't mean—" Red began, but William cut him off.

"I'm going home," William said, shaking his head sadly. "Maybe my Grandmama's right. Maybe I just don't belong here. It's too bad, because those meatballs were A-1."

William released the ball, pushing it in the direction of the two boys.

"Don't go," Tommy said. "We didn't mean to hurt your feelings."

William looked back and put up a hand. "Later, fellas," he said. "This nerd has to go home and study." And with that he turned his back on the boys and walked the two blocks back to his new house.

Two minutes later, William, deeply upset, strode up the flagstone path that led to his new front door. He repeatedly rang the bell and knocked hard, until he could hear his mother coming quickly to let him in.

"What happened?" she asked, as she unlocked and opened the door.

"Maybe I'm better off with the hoodlums," William growled. "At least they don't give me a hard time 'cause I'm black."

Adele, shocked, put a hand to her mouth.

"Where's my uniform?" William demanded.

"Your Grandmama's washing it," Adele said, mystified by the sudden change in her son's demeanor. "Did they say something to you? Did something happen?"

"I'm going to bed," William said, disgusted. He headed up the stairs without looking back.

Chapter 14

POSTER BOY

The next morning, William, still hurting from the conversation with Tommy and Red the night before, went back to school.

His uniform and books filled his backpack. He tried to put the whole thing behind him and give the school a fresh start. In all fairness, he decided, he *was* the only African-American most of these kids had ever met, as crazy as that seemed. They just needed to see that he was a regular kid, just like them. Give the whole thing time. People are people. They'd see that he was more than a basketball player.

William entered the school building at 7:50 am, ten minutes before the start of the school day. As was the case the previous morning, the principal, Principal Schmidt, was standing at the front door of the school wearing a shirt and tie, greeting the students.

When he saw William, his eyes lit up.

"Heard about how you lit up the gym in the practice yesterday," he told William, offering him a fist bump, which William reluctantly returned. "I know you'll be awesome when we play Martland tomorrow."

"Thanks," William said uneasily. "I'll do my best."

He looked up.

And that's when he saw the posters.

Overnight, someone had taken a photograph of William in his uniform at practice, tongue hanging out of his mouth just like Michael Jordan, having let fly a jumper from way beyond the arc.

Below his massive picture were the words:

"LUNCH MONEY!
LUNCH MONEY!
HE'S OUR MAN!
IF HE CAN'T BEAT MARTLAND
NO ONE CAN!
COME TO THE BIG GAME
FRIDAY, OCTOBER 10TH, 3:30 PM
TURNBERRY MIDDLE SCHOOL GYM!"

William stood there goggle-eyed, mouth open, shaking his head slowly, staring at the image of himself looking like a professional basketball player.

This wasn't cool.

Helplessly, he looked in both directions and saw that the same poster had been plastered to the walls of the school every twenty-five feet. He could see half a dozen images of himself as he stood in that one spot near the front door of the school.

Kids streaming by him to class stopped, pounded him on the back, offered him fist bumps and high fives, all smiling as they said his nickname. Girls batted their eyes and flipped their long ponytails at him.

"Hey, Lunch," said one pretty redhead. "I'm on cheer squad. Can't wait to see you tear it up out there." He was pretty sure he'd never seen that girl before, and he certainly didn't know her name.

William couldn't help but think of what his grandmother always said—don't let anyone call you out of your name.

It was one thing for the kids in his old neighborhood to call him "Lunch" or "Lunch Money." Or even Tommy or Red. They were cool.

But now...*everybody*?

William turned and quickly stepped out of the school, looking for Principal Schmidt, who was still in the same place, greeting students.

"You're a star!" Principal Schmidt said happily. "Do you love it?"

William shook his head.

"I don't want to be a star," he said apologetically. "I want to be a student."

"Of course you're a student," Principal Schmidt said, not understanding the real meaning of William's words. "You're a student here at Turnberry Middle School! And you just happen to be the biggest basketball sensation this school has ever had! Now everybody in the whole school knows who you are! I just thought that would be a really neat welcome for you."

"When I welcome somebody?" William said, trying to be polite, but inside he was panicked over the sudden, unexpected, and frankly undesired attention. "I just say, 'Welcome.' I don't put their pictures up all over the place. And I keep saying this, but nobody believes me. *I'm not that good.*"

Principal Schmidt just grinned.

"There's that trademark humility of yours," he said approvingly. "You can tell me you don't like the attention, but you better get used to it. I heard how you shot the lights out at practice yesterday. Coach Clark's out of his mind. The whole school is. You're a stud."

William shook his head.

"A stud is a horse," he replied, trying to keep his anxiety from running away with him. "I'm not a horse. I'm a twelve-year-old boy."

"I just wanted you to feel, you know, special," Principal Schmidt said, finally grasping that William was deeply embarrassed by the posters.

"I don't want to be special," William said politely, not wanting to hurt the principal's feelings or risk somehow getting thrown out of school for mouthing off. "Best thing I can possibly hope for is for people not to notice me. I'm new here. I'm just trying to fit in. It's hard enough, for obvious reasons. This—" He pointed back inside to the poster nearest the front door of the school. "—this makes it a million times harder."

Principal Schmidt thought for a minute. "It's going to look awfully strange if the posters come down," he said, sounding disappointed. "Some of the ladies in the PTA were up almost all night designing the poster and getting it printed. I don't want to let them down."

William looked helplessly at the poster.

"This is cray-cray," he said. "Look, Principal Schmidt, I know you're just trying to make me feel at home. And I know you're trying to get some school spirit going for the big game tomorrow. But I shouldn't be at the center of it! I've only been in the school twenty-four hours."

William remembered something.

"I'll tell you who should be on that poster," he said, speaking faster and faster, his panic rising. "Martin! That kid is the best point guard I've ever seen! He distributes the ball like he's Magic Johnson! He's the one who ought to be on the poster!"

The principal put his arm around William's shoulder.

"So well raised," the principal said, stopping to acknowledge a few entering girl students. "Look. William. The last thing I would want to do is make you uncomfortable. You go to homeroom. By the time you get out, the posters will be down. I promise."

William looked dejectedly into Principal Schmidt's eyes.

"That would be great," William agreed. "The only problem is, everybody's already seen them. It's gonna be like,

The Seattle Public Library

Columbia Branch

Visit us on the Web: www.spl.org

Checked Out Items 12/19/2018 16:29

XXXXXXXXX1005

Item Title	Due Date
0010091219229 Lunch Money can't shoot	1/9/2019

# of Items: 1

Renewals: 206-386-4190

TeleCirc: 206-386-9015 / 24 hours a day

Online: myaccount.spl.org

Pay your fines/fees online at pay.spl.org

why'd all the posters come down? It's probably just gonna raise more questions than it answers. Maybe we ought to just leave them up."

"Whatever you want, William," Principal Schmidt said, and his whole demeanor had changed as well. "It had never occurred to me that this might embarrass you. I just thought you might like the star treatment."

William bit his lip. "I was doing well enough as it was," he said. "The other kids are nice, the school's great, the teachers are better than any I've ever known, and even the cafeteria food is good. I just wish I could kind of ease into things instead of, well, this." He nodded at the poster one last time.

"I'll take them down," Principal Schmidt said. "As soon as homeroom begins. It was a mistake. I hope you'll forgive me."

William, speechless, looked into Principal Schmidt's eyes, trying to see if the principal was mocking him. William could never remember any authority figure, let alone a white authority figure, actually apologizing to him.

"It's all good," William said, his trademark smile finally returning to his face. "But I told you before and I'm telling you again! Yesterday in the gym? A fluke. A once-in-a-lifetime thing. I won't be dogging it tomorrow. It is exactly what I said. I'm just not that good."

"There I have to disagree with you," Principal Schmidt said, regaining his sense of authority and control.

"Then we'll have to agree to disagree," William said, quoting one of his mother's favorite sayings, "without being disagreeable."

Principal Schmidt grinned.

"Sounds like a plan."

William nodded, relieved that the confrontation had ended so well, and headed off to homeroom.

Chapter 15

AUTOGRAPH TIME

The conversation with the principal meant that Lunch Money got to homeroom just as the bell rang. He was worried that his homeroom teacher, Mr. Kenmore, would mark him tardy. At his old school, if you were tardy, you went to the principal's office, and the people there were so mean that kids figured they were better off not going to class at all. So they would just skip school altogether.

William sensed that the people who worked in the office at this school were nicer than the ones at his old school, but he didn't want to take a chance. He also realized that his sudden celebrity status meant that he could get away with almost anything.

At least until they figured out he couldn't ball.

As he let himself into the classroom, William was completely unprepared for the reception he received. A bunch of boys in the back row started rhythmically chanting, "*Lunch Money, Lunch Money*," clapping along. Pretty soon, the whole class had taken up the chant.

Eyes wide, William slowly made his way to his seat, as the cheering went on under the approving gaze of his teacher, Mr. Kenmore. *Amazing,* William thought. *Just yesterday, I was almost afraid of him. Now, I could do whatever I wanted and he wouldn't say a thing.*

Someone was tapping William on the shoulder.

It was the pretty girl with long, blonde hair who had looked so quizzically at him the day before.

"Can I have your autograph?" she asked.

Too embarrassed to say no, William scrawled "Lunch Money" on a sheet of composition paper with the pen that she had thrust into his hands. Soon, a sea of hands surrounded William, all wanting his autograph.

"Seems like we have a celebrity in the class today," Mr. Kenmore said, beaming.

William wanted to crawl in a hole. He glanced at the ground around his feet, hoping that a sudden earthquake or other natural disaster would occur at that moment, swallow him up and allow him a sudden escape from all the attention.

Not even his grandmother fussed over him like this.

"I'll give you my PlayStation," a boy was telling William. "I've got two. It's brand new. Just come over to my house after practice and let's hang out."

"My parents are taking us to the movies," another girl, almost as pretty as the one with blonde hair, told him. "Do you want to come?"

Is this still the sixth grade? William wondered. He nodded non-committal thanks to both offers and as quickly as he could made his way to his own seat.

Everybody stopped chanting his name and clapping.

The whole class was looking expectantly at him, as if he was suddenly going to pull a basketball out of his backpack and put on a one-man Harlem Globetrotters exhibition.

Or at least that was the way it felt to William.

"Pledge of allegiance," Mr. Kenmore said, and William was incredibly relieved. The announcements meant that attention in the class would shift from him to whatever was going on in the school.

He put his hand on his heart and recited the pledge along with the rest of the students, amazed that everyone seemed to be taking it seriously, unlike his last school, where half the class couldn't even bother to stand up.

"Thursday, October 9," said the student voice over the loudspeaker. "The PTA bake sale continues after school every day this week. Cookies and cake are available to support the 7th grade class trip to Washington, D.C.

"The book fair starts today and continues through Tuesday. Principal Schmidt expects 100 percent turnout from the student body for tomorrow's game against Martland Middle School at

3:30 in our school gym. Be sure to cheer for Turnberry's newest basketball sensation, William 'Lunch Money' Barnes.

"Have a great day."

William threw his head back and rolled his eyes. There was no escaping it.

"Would you like to share some of your strategy for tomorrow's game?" Mr. Kenmore asked.

William studied him. He seemed to be sincere. But why couldn't he understand that William was just dying on the inside with all this unwanted attention?

"I don't know if I have any strategy," William said modestly. "I just want to do a good job and represent."

The rest of the students burst into laughter. They started chanting, "Represent! Represent!" William, a puzzled expression on his face, had no idea why the word seemed so funny to them.

The students stopped chanting, and then burst into laughter and applause.

"Everybody heard about your performance at practice yesterday," Mr. Kenmore told William, as the rest of the class buzzed with excitement at the idea of having the school's hottest new celebrity in their midst.

"This is really embarrassing," William finally said, glancing at Tommy and Red, who just shrugged back. They understood William's embarrassment but they had no idea what to do about it.

"Nothing to be embarrassed about," Mr. Kenmore said. "You've got natural talent. A lot of people think the principal brought you in as a free agent from your other school, just to beat Martland."

Everybody laughed except William.

The words “natural talent,” when applied to an African-American athlete, just made him shake his head. You could be born with natural ability and still not be a star. White athletes were hard workers. Black athletes were just born that way.

But he wasn’t about to get into any of that in the classroom.

“I had a really lucky day in the gym yesterday,” he told the class, trying to find a way to dampen expectations for the next day’s game. “But the one thing I’ve said over and over since I got here, and nobody seems to be listening to it, is that I’m really not that good a basketball player.

“I have a Moms—a mom—who’s totally into making me study. And when she’s not home, my Grandmama does the same thing. I don’t have time to ball.

“I really have no idea what happened yesterday. It was like a freak thing. I just wish all of ya’ll would believe me when I tell you that basketball’s not my game.

“In fact, I don’t even know what my game is. But I know it ain’t—isn’t—hoops.”

And with that, William fell silent.

The room was silent now, as the students digested William’s words.

Mr. Kenmore, so stern yesterday, broke into an unexpected grin.

“That’s that humility I heard so much about from Principal Schmidt in the faculty meeting yesterday.” He beamed. “I think that just makes you even more special.”

William’s classmates burst into applause.

William rolled his eyes. They just weren’t getting it.

William was trying to figure out something else to say when, mercifully, the bell rang again, signaling the end of homeroom. Everybody excitedly grabbed their book bags, giving William more fist bumps, high fives, and even a couple of chest bumps.

This is crazy, William thought, as he got his own books together to prepare for first period.

What are these people going to do, he asked himself, *when they realize Lunch Money can't shoot?*

Chapter 16

ON THE HOUSE

In every class that morning, it was more of the same: celebratory high fives, fist bumps, chest bumps, requests for autographs, and invitations to hang out. William felt hollow. His great shooting the day before had placed expectations on him that he had no idea how he would live up to. In each class, he waited for the insanity to die down so that the teacher could finally just teach.

He dreaded lunch, because he knew his classmates would be unrestrained by teachers. He could barely get down the lunch line, loading his tray with meatloaf, which the other kids called mystery meat, although it looked pretty good to him. By the time he got to the cashier, to his amazement, a kid he didn't even know reached into his pocket, pulled out some crumpled bills, and paid for William's meal.

"Lunch Money," the boy said, "I've got your Lunch Money right here! Lunch is on me! You're gonna beat Martland!"

William just shook his head. Was this really happening? All he wanted to do was fit in. This was exactly the opposite.

Lunch Money murmured a shy thanks, picked up his tray, and scanned the cafeteria. All eyes were on him. He looked around for an empty table, but there were none. Fortunately, at that moment, Tommy and Red showed up.

"This is nuts," Tommy said, surveying the excited crowd of students, all clearly hoping that William would sit with them. Tommy sized up the situation and swiftly took control. "Come with us."

William, surprised, followed the two boys, also carrying trays, out the door to a quiet spot opposite the auditorium. There were no other students. They all sat down on the grass, their trays alongside them, and started to eat, William saying a hurried grace first.

"Are we allowed to do this?" William asked. "In my old school, if you took lunch trays out of the building, they'd think you were stealing them."

Red and Tommy looked at each other.

"We do this all the time," Tommy said.

Red nodded. "It's cool," he said, through a mouthful of meatloaf.

William sighed and took a bite of his food. "I never dreamt in a million years," he began thoughtfully, "that on my second day of school I'd have to hide from all the other kids."

"It happens," Tommy said. But none of the three boys could remember any other time when anything like this *had* ever happened.

"Sorry about last night," Red said.

William shook his head quickly.

"Forget about it," he said. "I'm the one who should apologize. I just got frustrated. Long day. Man, this meatloaf is good."

Red was about to disagree when Tommy glanced at him, cutting him off.

"Must have been cool, seeing your face on those posters," Tommy said instead. "You're an overnight sensation."

"A little bit," William admitted. "But I think I'd rather be up there for math or history."

"You're good at math?" Red asked, surprised.

"You think black people can't do math?" William asked, teasing him.

Red put his hands up and looked defensive.

"That's not what I meant," he said. "It's just because you're new."

"We had math at my old school," William said, "and I always loved it. But the math teacher wasn't great. Sometimes he didn't even show up to his own class."

Red and Tommy nodded.

"What's your school like?" Tommy asked.

"It's just...a school," William said, choosing his words carefully. "Like anywhere else. There's good kids and bad kids. Good teachers and bad teachers. You know how it is."

Red and Tommy nodded. William wondered what picture of an inner-city school the two boys were conjuring up in their minds.

He wanted to explain things in more detail, but he thought it would just make him feel even more different and alone. He changed the subject.

"Guys, I gotta tell you," William said. "I'm super nervous about the game tomorrow."

"I know, I know," Tommy said wearily. "You're not that good. We've only heard it a million times."

"Maybe you'll have a better game than you think," Red said encouragingly.

"Yeah, maybe," William said. "Or maybe everybody's gonna hate me when we lose."

"We always lose to Martland," Tommy said. "Nobody hates anybody."

"It's gonna be different this time," William replied. "I haven't even been with the team that long. I just had one practice. What are they expecting?"

"That thanks to you," Red said, "we're gonna beat a school we haven't beaten in twenty years, dude. And then we'll go on to win the county championship because we always see them in the finals. That's all."

"Don't let Red scare you," Tommy said. "You've got another practice today. There's still time to get out the jitters. And besides, if you shoot only half as well as you did yesterday, we'll win for sure."

William looked doubtful.

"The only question in my mind," he said, "is where I'm gonna move to after we lose."

"Life will go on," Tommy said. "It's just one game."

William shook his head. "Life will go on for *you*," he said. "For me, who knows. I'm just getting accustomed to the food here. It really is delicious."

Red and Tommy looked at each other doubtfully.

"Whatever you say," they chorused.

"You could always transfer to Martland," Red said, grinning. "If you help them win, they'll be happy to have you."

"Yeah," Tommy said, grinning. "Only the food there isn't good. You're gonna miss this. Five-star meatloaf, the nectar of the gods."

"Stop it," William said, but at least he was grinning. Maybe the whole thing would work out. He hoped.

Chapter 17

COLD AS ICE

By early afternoon, the excitement about Lunch Money and the sudden likelihood of finally beating Martland had died down to a mere tingle. Kids still stopped in their tracks and looked admiringly at William as he went by, but the energetic fist bumps, shoulder bumps, and in one over-excited case a head bump, gave way to a more subdued sense of respect and wonder. Who was this kid who had dropped into their world from another planet? It didn't matter. All that mattered was that he could shoot.

When the school day ended, William headed for the gymnasium and the boys' locker room to change into his uniform, which his Grandmama had washed by hand the night before and had pressed to perfection. He wondered what magic lamp he might have inadvertently rubbed prior to yesterday's practice, releasing the genie who granted him the ability to ball.

He wondered whether he could find that same lamp before today's practice.

No such luck.

Coach Clark started practice with the boys running a couple of laps around the playground and then brought them inside for shooting drills. Nobody really wanted to shoot. All anybody wanted to do was watch William shoot. So the practice was less of a real practice and instead, all present, even Coach Clark, looked expectantly at William, as if he were going to put on a private clinic for those lucky enough to be present. Even Martin, who did not want to risk another tongue lashing from William, was subdued. There was only one problem.

William's shooting touch had grown cold.

Not cool summer evening cold.

Ice cold.

Meat locker cold.

Cold enough to freeze liquid natural gas.

That cold.

William knew it even before the first shot left his hand. He clanged an easy layup off the rim and then missed his next nine layups, only hitting his eleventh, not that anyone was counting.

That's more like it, William thought grimly.

Everybody else figured he was starting slowly. William knew he wasn't. He was going to be slow in the middle and even slower at the end.

Coach Clark didn't look overly concerned. He blew his whistle and had the kids work on passing drills, primarily to give William a chance to calm down so that he could find his shot. After five minutes of passing, the coach blew his whistle again and had the kids work on shooting from the top of the key. Once again, it quickly turned into a William-fest, with the other kids basically passing the ball to William and waiting for the magic to happen.

It never happened. William whiffed. William fanned. William missed. William tossed up air balls. William looked like he couldn't find the basket with a roadmap, GPS, or a seeing-eye dog.

After ten minutes of this, Coach Clark and William's teammates were exchanging curious glances. What the heck had happened to their star?

William knew what had happened—he had simply gone back to being the William he knew he was. The kid picked last.

Coach Clark blew his whistle again and had the boys work on foul shooting. Maybe that will settle William down, he thought, assuming that William was feeling way too much pressure in only a second day on the team. It had to be tough to go from new kid in school to basketball savior in twenty-four short hours.

The team, for its part, had begun to lose interest in William and instead started trying to find their own shots. Whether William made or missed his foul shots was of little consequence to the rest of the team. They started to focus on their own foul shooting.

The William Show, for at least one day, was over.

Tommy shot William a curious glance when he was finally able to make eye contact, since William was keeping his head down when he wasn't looking up at the basket. William responded with a quick shrug, as if to say, your guess is as good as mine. Behind Tommy, Red flashed him a thumbs-up sign and a goofy grin.

Practice went on for another forty-five minutes. William put up as many shots as the rest of the kids, but made practically none. Practice couldn't end quickly enough for him. As soon as the coach blew the final whistle, he practically flew off the court.

In the locker room, William changed as quickly as he could, because he didn't want to have to discuss his miserable performance with the rest of the team. He shoved his uniform in his backpack and hightailed it out of the locker room, only to be called back by the sound of Coach Clark's voice.

"William," Coach Clark said evenly, and William tried to figure out what the sound of his tone meant. He wasn't sure, but then, Coach Clark wasn't quite sure of anything, either.

William, head down, walked slowly from the door of the locker room to Coach Clark's tiny office.

The coach sat himself down and pointed to a folding chair opposite his desk.

For a long time, no one spoke.

"Tough practice today, Lunch Money," Coach Clark said in a voice that was neither kind nor unkind.

It sounded to William as if the coach was looking for an explanation.

"I really stunk up the joint," William said, not looking up.

Coach Clark nodded.

"The whole school put way too much pressure on you," he said, sounding sad and a little embarrassed. "Principal Schmidt, me, everybody."

William shrugged as if to say, you got that right.

"You're a good kid," Coach Clark said.

"Thank you, sir," William said.

"Well raised, too," the coach added.

William nodded again, as if to give thanks for the praise, but he was thinking, how come everybody says I'm well raised? Are they surprised when an African-American kid has manners? Do they think we're all gangsters and rappers?

"What are you thinking about?" the coach asked perceptively.

"Nothing," William lied.

"It can't be easy," the coach said. "It's tough enough to come into a new school. On top of that, you're our first bl— um, African-American. And then on top of that, everybody's expecting you to win the game for us tomorrow."

William shrugged again.

"Three for three," he said ruefully. "Your average is a lot better than mine today."

"Can I ask you a question?" Coach Clark said, leaning forward.

"Sure," William said, as if he had any choice in the matter.

"It just doesn't add up to me," Coach Clark said slowly. "How you could've played so well yesterday and, well, not so well today."

"Is that a question?" William asked, finally looking up at the coach.

Coach Clark bit his lip. "Maybe not," he said. "Let me try that again. Are you...mad at me?"

William blinked.

"Coach, are you suggesting I dogged it out there today?" he asked, surprised and hurt.

Now it was the coach's turn to shrug.

"Honestly, Lunch—I mean William, I'm not quite sure what else to think."

William stared in disbelief at the coach.

"Let me get this straight," he said, struggling to hold back his emotions. "You thought that I *missed* all those shots on *purpose*? Because I was angry that everybody was turning me into some sort of basketball star?"

"You did put on some display yesterday," Coach Clark said cautiously. He realized he should never have said what he had been thinking.

"So that's what you believe," William said, giving a sad, slight shake of his head. "And then you tell me I was well raised. It's one or the other, Coach, isn't it? If I was well raised, I wouldn't be dogging it on the basketball court, letting my teammates down, just to make a point. Am I right?"

Coach Clark thought for a long time before he responded.

Finally he gave a small, reluctant nod.

"You're right," he said. "That's what I thought."

"That's what I thought you thought," William said, and he reached in his backpack and took out his uniform.

"I think this belongs to you," he said sadly, and he put the powder blue jersey and shorts on the coach's desk.

The coach stared guiltily at the uniform. He knew he had really blown it.

"Think it over," the coach said. "You don't have to decide right now."

William stood, his decision final. "I think *you* best think it over," he said softly.

He zipped up his backpack, stood, turned, and stepped out of Coach Clark's office.

Chapter 18

TAKE ME HOME

As soon as his mother opened the front door of their house, William stepped inside and tossed his backpack toward the dining room table with such force that it skidded off the table onto the floor.

William, head down, ignored the fallen backpack and instead headed straight up the stairs to his room, without even saying a word.

His mother watched him go. She waited a few minutes to allow William to compose himself, and then she went upstairs and knocked softly on his door.

No answer.

Adele opened the door a crack and saw William sitting sullenly on his bed, staring into space.

"May I come in?" she said.

"Suit yourself," William said, still not looking up at her.

"What happened, William?" Adele asked, her voice soft and soothing.

William shook his head. "Just take me back to the 'hood, Moms," he said quietly. "This is no place for the likes of you and me."

Adele stared at him.

"What happened?" she asked, swallowing hard.

William recounted the events of the day. How there were posters of him all over the school. And then how everybody was treating him like a rock star. And then how he lost his shooting touch in the practice, which came as no surprise to him, since he still hadn't figured out how he'd gotten his touch in the first place the day before. And then finally the confrontation with the coach, and the accusation that William had chosen not to play his best just to teach his coach and teammates some kind of lesson.

"I quit the team," William concluded. "Gave Coach back the uniform. I didn't want this kind of attention. I didn't want *any* attention."

Adele looked sadly at her son. That was the hard thing about hard things, she thought. Even when times were good, that didn't make them easy.

"I feel for you, son," Adele said.

Beatrice stuck her head in the door.

"Not now, Mama," Adele said gently to her mother.

"I just want to see if the boy is hungry," Beatrice said.

"Maybe later, ma'am," William said.

"That boy's well raised," Beatrice said approvingly.

"That's what everybody says," William said, with a trace of bitterness.

"They say that because it's true," Beatrice said. "Mm, mm, mm."

She stepped away and a moment later they heard her going down the stairs.

"You can't quit," Adele said quietly.

"I *have* to quit," he said sadly. "Take me back to the 'hood. At least there, they treat me bad because that's just how they treat people. Somehow it's worse when it's all about the color of your skin."

Adele sighed.

"I brought you up here," she began, "because I wanted to shield you from what goes on in the world. But I can't. Not there, not here."

William thought about what his mother said and nodded.

"The world is the world," he said. "I just don't know where I'm supposed to be in it. Up there with the hoodlums? Down here with the people who don't know who I am? Who make assumptions, based on what they see? Where do I belong? Isn't there some kind of nice suburb with just black folk? Can't we go live there?"

Adele thought about it.

"There are such neighborhoods," she said. "I don't think your Uncle has a house in any of them, though. It would take a little bit of time before we can find a place and move there."

"It's all the same to me," William said, shaking his head. "I'm sure there'd people who would look down on us because we don't have as much money as some of them. It just seems like we can't win."

"That's not what I raised you to believe," Adele said quietly.

"Then what *should* I believe?" William asked. "In fairy tales? In superheroes? In magic?"

"I brought you up," Adele said, still quietly, "to believe in yourself."

William looked annoyed.

"Like I really need a fortune cookie slogan right now," he said.

Adele softened.

"I'm sorry," she said. "I hate seeing you suffering like this." She paused. "You really want to move back?"

William shrugged.

"I want to give this place a chance," he said. "But I want *them* to give *me* a chance. Not treat me like I'm some sort of basketball god. Just because I'm black. Just treat me like a new kid. Ignore me. Steal my Lunch Money. But just let me *be*."

Adele thought about it.

"That doesn't sound like too much to ask," she agreed. "Should we go see the principal tomorrow? The two of us?"

William thought about it. "Moms, you gotta get to work. You can't keep taking days off. Not in this economy."

Adele laughed. "What do you know about 'this economy'?"

"You talk about it all the time," William said. "'I can't do *this* in this economy. I can't do *that* in this economy.' I don't even know what that means. All I know is, you gotta go back to your job. You can't keep hanging around here, waiting to see what happens next with me at that school."

Adele thought about it and nodded.

"Okay," she said.

"I'll go talk to Principal Schmidt myself," William said. "Time for me to man up."

Adele suppressed a grin at the idea of her twelve-year-old son "manning up."

"And what will you tell Principal Schmidt?" she asked.

"I don't know," William admitted. "But you'd best believe I'll tell him *something*."

Adele thought about it for a moment and rose. "You do just that," she said. "I'll tell Grandmama to hold supper until you come down."

Adele reached for her son and held him. They both held back tears.

William nodded thanks and watched his mother head out of the room.

Chapter 19

LESSONS

The next morning, as William approached the entrance to the school, he saw Principal Schmidt standing in his usual spot, greeting the students.

"I need to talk to you," William told the principal.

"I need to talk to you, too," the principal said, studying William. "Meet me in my office. I'll be there in ten minutes."

William nodded and headed into the school building. Instead of going to his homeroom, he headed for Principal Schmidt's office.

William told the women in the office that he and Principal Schmidt were going to speak, and they told him to go right ahead and sit down in one of the chairs opposite Principal Schmidt's desk. William did so, glancing around at the now-familiar faces, mostly white, peering down at him.

A few minutes later, Principal Schmidt came in. Instead of sitting at his desk, he sat in a chair across from William.

"I heard about your conversation with Coach Clark yesterday," Principal Schmidt said.

William nodded. "I'd like to go back on the team," he said seriously.

Principal Schmidt looked quickly at William.

"It looked like you quit for all time," he said cautiously. "What changed?"

William thought for a moment.

"Maybe *I* did," he said.

Principal Schmidt waited.

"My mom always says," William continued, "'If the situation doesn't change, you change.' I don't think the coach is a bad man," he said, choosing his words carefully. "I don't think you are, either."

"Well, thanks," Principal Schmidt said, looking relieved. "I thought you didn't have too much use for me by now."

"I just think you made some decisions about me," William continued, "before you knew anything about me."

Principal Schmidt reddened. They both knew it was true.

"I kept telling you over and over that I can't ball," William continued. "But nobody believed me.

"All my teachers speak to me loudly and slowly, like I come from some other country where they don't speak English.

"I'm actually really good at math. And social studies. And English. I bet I'd be good at science, but my school didn't really have science. I don't think they could afford all that lab stuff.

"Tell the teachers I understand English just fine. Will you do that?"

Principal Schmidt nodded quickly.

"I can do that," he said.

William thought for another moment and went on.

"And please don't put up any more posters of me," he said. "I didn't come here to beat Martland. I've never heard of Martland. I just came here to go to school and get away from the hoodlums in my old neighborhood.

"I don't want special treatment. I don't want *any* treatment. I just want to...go to school. Make friends. Do homework." He grinned. "Eat lunch."

"I get it," the principal said. "I owe you an apology. You're right about everything you've said. Every word."

William gave a small nod.

"Don't sweat it," William said. "Let bygones be bygones. But seriously. I do want to play for the team."

Principal Schmidt looked perplexed.

"You've made clear to me that you can't play well," he said. "So why would you want to play?"

William grinned.

"I didn't say I don't like to play," William corrected him. "I just said I'm not very good. In my neighborhood? I would never have had a chance if my life depended on it. Over here, this is a team I think I could make. I *think*."

The principal thought about it.

"It's up to the coach," he said.

William shook his head.

"It's up to you," he said politely but firmly. "Coach Clark works for you. He'll do whatever you tell him. I'd like to go back on the team."

"William, you're a remarkable young man," Principal Schmidt said admiringly.

"Just as long as you don't call me well raised," William said evenly. "I think that line's been done to death."

Principal Schmidt nodded again.

"In a school, the teachers and the administrators are supposed to teach the kids. In your case, I think it's been the other way around."

They sat quietly for a moment, and suddenly the bell went off, announcing the beginning of homeroom.

"You'll be late for homeroom," Principal Schmidt said. "I'll write you a note."

"That won't be necessary," William said. "I'll just tell Mr. Kenmore I was talking to you."

Principal Schmidt nodded. He rose and offered his hand to William, who shook it.

"You're a good kid, Lunch Money," the principal said. "If it's okay I call you that."

William grinned. "It's okay," he said.

"And welcome back to the basketball team."

William released the principal's hand, looked at him in the eye, nodded, and headed out of the office on his way to homeroom.

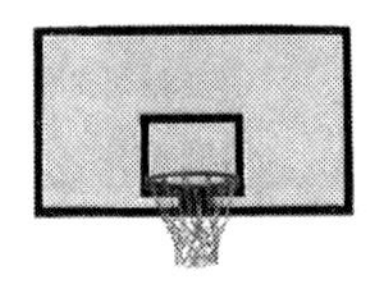

Chapter 20

THE NOT SO BIG GAME

For the rest of the day, the atmosphere at Turnberry Middle School returned to its pre-Lunch Money state of normalcy. Classes went on, kids ate lunch, they joked and teased in the hallways, and people mostly let William be.

For his part, William went about his business, raising his hand when he thought he knew the answer to a question, minding his own business the rest of the time. He ate his lunch in the cafeteria with Red and Tommy. Nobody asked for his autograph.

When the last bell rang at 3:00, William headed to the boys' locker room to retrieve his uniform from Coach Clark, who was fine with him coming back on the team. He changed and got ready for the big game against Martland.

Martin started at point guard. William started on the bench. By halftime, Martland was winning by thirteen points.

By the end of the third quarter, Martland was up by seventeen.

Coach Clark finally put William into the game with four minutes to go in the fourth quarter and Martland up by twenty.

William took three shots, and made one.

Turnberry Middle School lost big, but nobody seemed to mind.

The End

ABOUT THE AUTHORS

MICHAEL LEVIN

Twice a *New York Times* Bestselling Author, Michael Levin has written credibly and effectively about race on numerous occasions, including the national bestseller *Dropping the Ball* with Baseball Hall of Famer Dave Winfield (Simon and Schuster), in *No Ordinary Love* with NBA star Doug and Jackie Christie, with civil rights leader and ambassador to the United Nations John Hope Bryant in national bestseller *Banking On Our Future* (Beacon Press), and most recently for Politico.com—*Shoveling While Black*, a story about former baseball star and ESPN commentator Doug Glanville, who was racially profiled in his own driveway while shoveling snow.

He is also married to a woman born in mainland China and is raising four mixed-race children, including 12-year-old twins who have been a sounding board throughout the creation of the Lunch Money series.

Levin is also the author of two young adult novels. *Janine and Alex, Alex and Janine*, a young adult novel published by Putnam/Berkley and made into an ABC Sunday Night Disney Movie of the Week, *Model Behavior. Model Behavior* aired twice on ABC and has appeared countless times on the Disney Channel. Its companion novel, *Sam and Derek, Derek and Sam* was also optioned by a leading producer but was not made.

Levin has written, created, or edited eleven national bestsellers. Two of the books he wrote have been profiled on *60 Minutes*. His work has received outstanding reviews in *The New Yorker*, *The New York Times* (daily and Sunday), *People Magazine*, *Newsweek*, *Esquire*, *The Washington Post, The Los Angeles Times, The Cleveland Plain Dealer*, and many other top outlets.

His work has been optioned and/or made by Disney, HBO, ABC, Stephen Soderbergh, Darren Star, Paramount, among others.

He writes an online column in the New York Daily News and blogs regularly about books and publishing for Huffington Post.

Levin has four children, age fifteen down to eight, of whom three are already book authors.

JACK PANNELL

Jack J. Pannell, Jr. is the founder and organizer of the Baltimore Collegiate School for Boys, an urban, college prep charter school expected to open in Fall, 2015. Mr. Pannell is the President of the Five Smooth Stones Foundation, Inc., a non-profit organization he founded with a mission to transform a generation of urban boys with world-class educational opportunities. In developing Baltimore Collegiate as a charter school project, Mr. Pannell visited and studied over thirty high performing schools in the county and also spent a year of teaching at St. Ignatius, a Jesuit middle school for boys in Baltimore and at Collington Square Elementary School, one of the lowest performing schools in Maryland.

Mr. Pannell is the former Executive Director of the Baltimore Curriculum Project, a charter school management organization that operates four charter schools in East Baltimore. With over fifteen years of non-profit and government leadership experience, he has held senior management positions with Episcopal Diocese of Maryland, Sojourners and the Department of Health for the District of Columbia. During his time in Washington D.C., Mr. Pannell was the communication director for Congressman John Lewis (D-Georgia) and Senator Harry Reid (D-Nevada). Prior to working in Washington, Mr. Pannell worked in the entertainment and investment banking industries. He is a graduate of Amherst College and Loyola Law School, Los Angeles.

CPSIA information can be obtained
at www.ICGtesting.com
Printed in the USA
LVOW08s1056210617
538825LV00007B/114/P